THE
CANVAS ADVENTURES

BY

T. G. BRYANT

DEDICATION

This book is dedicated to all the magnificent people who help make life beautiful.

- T. G.

TABLE OF CONTENTS

PART ONE

"At the center of the Universe is a loving heart that continues to beat and that wants the best for every person. Anything that we can do to help foster the intellect and spirit and emotional growth of our fellow human beings, that is our job. Those of us who have this particular vision must continue against all odds. Life is for service."

- FRED ROGERS

CHAPTER ONE

Sameness

Harmony prided itself on sameness. Not one family unit was different. Every family had two children and one mother and one father. This was the law in Harmony that was never questioned. If any family units were found in violation, they would be banished from Harmony and never allowed back. No one knew where rule breakers were sent, and no one ever asked.

There was a certain charm about Harmony, but none of it was real. Hidden beneath the façade of happy residents, rooted a secret. It was no secret, however, that Harmony demanded sameness, and it was no secret why this was the case, either.

Those who lived in Harmony saw it as a privilege to live in such a perfect, idyllic place. It was a second chance for its residents. The sameness wasn't seen as a law but a way of life. Harmony's people found that sameness was important for blending in and making sure everyone had equal footing in society. They didn't believe in competition. Instead, Harmony's leaders believed in creating a utopian society. One where nothing changed, including its leadership. Unfortunately, Harmony's society wasn't a utopian but a dystopian.

The leaders of Harmony didn't believe in differences in any form, whether it be differences of opinion, belief, or government. Even the people living in Harmony looked similar. Everything was decided for them, and no one dared to question this model for living. Ever.

In Harmony, all the houses were built to the same scale, and all the cars were the same make and model. If you could find a difference in Harmony, it would be the colors of the homes and cars. Even then, the choices were simple: black or white. The streets had simple names like Main,

Maple, and Elm, and all roads circled back together at the Harmony Municipal Building.

Yes, all those who lived in Harmony lived in peace and, well, harmony. There was no crime, and there was no time for parties. Most celebrations, particularly birthdays, were nonexistent. There weren't any teenagers getting into shenanigans on weekends because there were little chances for trouble. Harmony's mayor, Norm Hull, or, Mayor Norm as he liked to be called, was always running unopposed because the residents knew he was the only one for the job. No one dared to defy his authority. Ever.

Norm Hull was a heavy, short man with very little hair. The few hairs he had left on his scalp were greying. He would often ride through Harmony to check on residents and knock on doors to give out buttons to encourage people to vote for him. He would visit people in their homes to talk about the upcoming elections to ensure he had their vote even though he ran unopposed. He rather liked his name as he felt it made him sound like a normal person.

His name represented his demand for sameness. He thought of himself as better than any resident.

In truth, Mayor Hull was as crooked as many other politicians, but the citizens of Harmony didn't care. They were too concerned with their own lives and respecting their powerful leader to ever question him or anything else about Harmony.

Mayor Hull's office was filled with loyal followers. They were afraid of him despite his small stature. His small stature never prevented him from commanding a room. He was never a victim of bad press as he owned all the newspapers, radio and television stations. He staffed each with journalists who never sought truth but harmony. Harmony's council members acted as loyal minions, almost like pirates, because they always voted his way. All votes were unanimous, because no one ever dissented to Mayor Hull's proposals.

However, like any other place, Harmony's residents had secrets. At least one family, anyway. This family unit didn't follow the orders of Mayor Hull. They broke the law, but no one else knew. This was not the family's wish or choice. Instead, an outside force thrust the law breaking upon them, and it began long, long ago...

CHAPTER TWO

Twelve Years Ago

The two men arrived on the long, dark, and lonely street just after 2 o'clock in the morning when everyone in Harmony was fast asleep. The only sounds were crickets in the grass and owls in the trees. The two didn't belong here and if found, they would stick out due to their obvious differences from Harmony's residents.

One man carried a large oil canvas painting and the other carried a basket with something inside. They whispered to one another as they passed house after house, looking for the right one.

"Are you sure we are doing the right thing?" the shorter one asked. He was dark in complexion and dressed in a multi-colored robe. His eyes twinkled under the streetlights. He often spoke with an excited tone. But not tonight. No, tonight, the smaller man was afraid. He wasn't afraid for himself but for someone else.

"Of course we are!" the taller one replied. "We have no choice anyway," he continued. The man was very thin and looked to be one hundred years old or more. His skin was pale and leathery, yet he walked with the speed of a man half his age. He wore a heavy, dark robe that seemed to sparkle any time the two passed streetlights.

"This place gives me the creeps!" the shorter one said to the other. He pulled his robe tighter for warmth, but he wasn't cold. "Look! I'm getting goosebumps! Did you notice how all the houses are exactly the same? Come on, let's go back! He's not part of this World. He belongs in our World! Not here!" He knew in his heart he had to follow orders, however.

"Hush!" the older man scolded him. "It's not up for discussion! The King sent us to protect the boy's safety, and he's safer here than back home, especially after what happened."

The shorter man knew his friend was right. Only hours ago, he'd been given the orders from The King. This didn't stop the shorter man from glaring at the taller man, "How *exactly* is he safer here?"

He was quickly cut off by the older one. "That's enough!"

The two grew closer and closer to their destination, and as they did, they grew more and more frightened. The shorter man looked down at the basket. The contents inside began to make a startling cry. He stopped and peeled back a blanket, revealing an infant baby boy. The man smiled at the baby and softly whispered, "It's okay. We're almost there! We're not going to let anything happen to you!" At that moment, the shorter man waved his hand over the boy's head, and the baby instantly stopped crying. He was soothed by the man's touch. The shorter man smiled brightly with pride over this action.

"I wish you wouldn't use your magic in this World. Someone could see you!" The older man scolded him and waved a finger in his friend's face.

The shorter man groaned. "People are asleep! This could be the last time I get to use it with him," he replied, snapping back with his own finger, which paled in size.

The older man rolled his eyes. Despite the annoyance, he knew the other was right. The two men then continued down the street. Finally, after several miles of road, they reached their destination.

"Well, here we are: 3000 Elm Street," the shorter man said while clutching the basket nervously and turning to the older man. "We can still turn around and take him home, you know?" When he didn't get a reply from his friend, he tried again, "So, that's a yes?"

The older man shook his head, but it was obvious he was thinking about it, too. "No. King's orders, I'm sorry." He appeared to be apologizing to himself and not the other man. He tightened his grip on the oil canvas painting he held in his hand.

After considering their options, the two made their way up the driveway toward the dark, ugly house. They exchanged looks briefly as if they were somehow hoping to convince the other that what they were about to do was wrong and not the right decision. The moment never came, however.

When they finally reached the doorstep, the shorter man hesitated but eventually put the basket down and sighed heavily. The older man followed with the oil canvas painting. Taking a large envelope from his robe, he put it inside the basket.

"Well..." the older man began, holding back tears and clearing his throat.

"Well..." the shorter man nodded but never added to his sentence. It was obvious neither man wanted to leave the scene. They stared at the basket and the oil canvas painting for what seemed like a long time. However, it was only a few seconds.

Eventually, the older man bent down and looked into the basket and tucked the blanket tighter to cover up the boy. "Goodbye, little guy. When the time is right, we will see you again."

The two knew, however, that the day might never happen at all. The shorter man bent down as well and looked into the basket to say his goodbyes. "Goodbye, Gabriel."

With their goodbyes now said, the two men turned to one another, nodded, sighed in defeat, and walked down the driveway.

Then they vanished into the night.

CHAPTER THREE

Present Day

He was different than any other resident of Harmony, and the Canton family reminded him of this fact daily. That is why they locked him in a small room, far away from the other members of the family. Mort made sure no one could see him, so he had the bedroom's windows boarded up so Mayor Norm Hull would never find Gabriel. After all, having a third child was against the law. They couldn't allow anyone to find out they had him. He was treated differently, too. Compared to the rest of the family, Gabriel was unique. If there was any love to be shared, the little boy never felt it in his heart. It was never shown to him. He was a loner and had no friends.

Mort and Marge Canton were a happy couple and wanted to remain in Harmony with their two children, Gretel and Gus, but having someone like Gabriel threatened that peace and harmony daily. Their peace and harmony was interrupted by Gabriel's arrival long ago...

Mort discovered Gabriel twelve years ago on his doorstep and was thankful none of the neighbors noticed him first. The contents of the envelope were quickly read and explained that Gabriel was to remain with them by order of The King. This was an inconvenience to say the least.

"I don't understand!" Marge said to Mort when he read the letter to her as she held the baby in her arms, unable to stop him from crying. She didn't have the same success of the shorter man from earlier. "Hush! Quiet, Nephew," she hissed at him. Marge had the maternal power of a cobra snake.

Mort continued to read the letter. "It appears something has happened to your sister and brother-in-law." He glossed over further details regarding their condition before adding, "And The King feels he'll be safer here with us!"

Marge rolled her eyes and groaned, "Oh, for goodness sake! Don't they know we have laws here in Harmony? We can't take him. I didn't even want the first two!"

Mort skimmed over the letter and cleared his throat, "I don't think we have a choice." He stared at the boy and grunted, annoyed. "Looks like you're going to live with us, Mutt." He rubbed the baby's head, and Gabriel immediately began crying even louder. Mort's brow furrowed.

That day was not a pleasant memory for Mort and Marge. Gabriel's aunt and uncle constantly reminded him how much of an inconvenience he was for breaking their perfect harmony ever since. He wasn't special to them. He was a nuisance. A nuisance Marge vowed she'd one day end.

Mort worked as a watch and jewelry salesman and prided himself on selling watches that only worked for a few months. He called himself the best salesman in Harmony. He never sold to the residents of Harmony, however. That was his specialty. He sold his watches and jewelry to people online under different names so he couldn't be tracked down or jailed for his crimes. Mort was a tall man and had a large black mustache that he often had to color because he thought it made him look younger. It didn't. His brow furrowed any time he was upset or felt uncomfortable.

Marge was a housewife that never did any housework. She claimed she did work when Mort was away, but in reality, she would go out during the day, and leave Gabriel to do the work on her behalf. Marge was short and thin but had a long neck that she used to spy on her neighbors nearby. She loved gossiping about others but believed all her personal affairs were no one else's business. It was her own defense mechanism at having such a terrible secret living in her home.

Gretel and Gus never got into any trouble at Harmony High School, but that's not because they were well-behaved. They were good at covering their tracks. Gus was often the ringleader in their pranks and foolishness. The truth: they were no better than their parents and never got caught. Gretel looked like her mother and Gus like his father.

Indeed, Gabriel was nothing like the rest of his family. His skin was fair in tone and he had pale blue eyes and beautiful blond hair. The rest of his family had dark, brown eyes. Not pretty brown eyes that some people have. The Canton's brown eyes seemed to stare back in terrifying, intimidating ways. Some might call them 'eyes of coal,' but Gabriel's eyes in contrast, were pure and angelic. He was also very smart, but there was nothing smart about the rest of his family.

Unlike Gretel and Gus, Gabriel loved to learn. The only problem was Gabriel was never allowed to attend school. He had to do all of his learning by watching educational programming on television when his family left the house.

Every morning, Marge would attempt to make breakfast, despite her hatred for all housework, and would call Gus and Gretel to the table. She loved her family but would never call Gabriel to the table. He would only get what was left from the meal. The family ate together and never discussed him unless he caused what they determined to be trouble the day before. This was often the case.

One morning, Mort poured a cup of coffee and looked across the table at Gus and Gretel. "Everything going well at school lately, my children?" he asked as he ate his eggs messily. He often missed his mouth as he shoved food inside it. Some of the yolk from his eggs dripped into his mustache.

The children stared at their father for a moment but nodded and ate quietly. Marge turned her attention from the stove to a small room after she heard rustling sounds from the inside. This room belonged to Gabriel.

"He's up!" Gus declared with a groan.

Gretel stared at the room and bit her lip. She appeared nervous. "Should we let him out?"

Marge quickly ignored the concerns of the family. "Don't worry about it. He knows he can't come out of there until after we're all out of the house. I'll bring him his meal when I leave for the day. Just eat." Gretel continued to stare, and her mother snapped a finger at her daughter. "Gretel, that means you, too!"

Gretel nodded and ate as the sounds continued and were getting louder with each passing moment. Both Gretel and Gus turned their heads toward the closed door and then turned their heads to one another. Gretel fidgeted from under the table clutching her fist.

Mort was now finished with his meal. He soon moved on to trying to busy himself by reading his morning paper. He quickly put it down and cleared his throat. "Just ignore him, Children. He's only doing this for attention."

Gretel and Gus nodded, and Gretel's fist relaxed.

Eventually the noises stopped. The entire family appeared to breathe a sigh of relief.

"See?" Mort pointed out to his children. "Now, hurry along or you'll be late for school." Gretel and Gus protested for a moment but were quickly hushed by their parents.

Mort and Marge hurried their children out the door. As Mort watched them walk down the street, he turned to Marge. He had a look of panic on his face. "Marge! We've got to do something about that boy!" Mort shouted as he pointed to Gabriel's pathetic excuse for a bedroom. "I'm tired of him worrying our children. What if they find out where he's from?"

Marge laughed as she refilled her husband's coffee cup. She nearly forced her husband to sit by pushing him. "Oh, Mort, always one to worry. Now, drink your coffee. Then you'll need to get on with your day, my love. You need to make some money for the family." She patted her husband's back and smiled.

Mort always felt he should press the matter further but after drinking his wife's coffee, he, perhaps, magically, changed his mind. His wife was right about one thing. He did have a meeting to sell a few watches to an online distributor. So, as he often did, he caved to his wife's demands, "If you say so, Dear."

Soon, the house was empty, and Gabriel was left alone as he always was on days like today. However, today was different. Today, Gabriel had a plan.

CHAPTER FOUR

The Key

Marge was always the last one to leave 3000 Elm Street. As she left, she made sure all the rooms in the house were locked and all the curtains closed. This was because she didn't want Gabriel to go into any of the rooms. He was forbidden from entering any room with a window, at least while the family was around. Gabriel didn't know why there was a need for such a thing, but he didn't dare question his aunt and uncle. Marge knew why, however. She understood all too well. If the family was found in violation of the two-child policy, they would be banished from Harmony.

Just before 8:30 that morning, Gabriel heard a quick knock on his door, followed by the front door opening and then closing again. He timidly opened the door and saw a plate of food. Today, he received a piece of dry toast, one egg, half a piece of bacon, and a glass of water. He ate the food quickly because he didn't know how much time he had before Aunt Marge would return. He wanted to make sure he had time to execute his plan. He'd been hoping for an opportunity, and recently he was given a chance!

Only the day before, unknown to anyone else, his aunt left a key behind on the kitchen counter. Gabriel knew that this was of course, was not intentional on his aunt's part. She was always very careful about locking doors and taking all keys with her. Always. Gabriel didn't discover this until after everyone left, and he wasn't sure if the key would open any of the doors. However, just the idea of knowing it might open one of the doors in the house excited Gabriel. He'd never seen any of the rooms in the house other than the kitchen, living room, and, of course, his prison of a bedroom.

The young boy was eager to see something, anything, other than the room he felt like a prisoner in for the last twelve years! Gabriel noticed the key sitting on the counter and quickly swiped it and put it under his pillow on his small cot to hide it from his family. He told himself that the next day would be the perfect opportunity to try the key out.

Gabriel rinsed out his plate and loaded it in the dishwasher, along with all the other members of his family's dishes. It was his job to clean up after them every morning. Once he finished, he walked to the living room and cleaned up that area, too. He was also responsible for making sure the living room was tidy. After all, Marge was not a good housewife. She led her family to believe she did the chores, when, in truth, it was Gabriel.

Once the house was back in order to Marge's liking, Gabriel went back to his room to retrieve the key. He pulled back his pillow and clutched the brass item in his hand and smiled. For a moment, he just stared at the key and wondered if searching for the door it opened was a good idea. He'd played it safe for years, but then after talking it over with his inner conscience, he knew what he had to do.

"Today is the day," Gabriel said. "I don't know if I'm going to find anything worth my time, but my life changes today!" He then shook his head, "No. Correction! My adventure begins today!"

He had no idea how right he was.

CHAPTER FIVE

What He Found

Gabriel exited his small bedroom and passed a few doors. He figured he would start at the end of the hall and work his way back. He felt both nervous and excited.

He held the key in his hand and stopped at the first door in the long, narrow hallway. He took the key, slid it into the slot and turned the handle. The key fit, but it didn't work for the door. "Shoot!" Gabriel exclaimed and moved on to the second door and repeated the process with similar results.

When he reached the third door, however, he felt a different energy as soon as he saw it. For starters, the door looked like it hadn't been opened in a long, long time. He gripped the door handle tightly in his hand. He slid the key into the slot, heard a loud click, and something weird happened. The key turned itself!

Gabriel stood back. He was afraid to move. He watched it happen as he took yet another step back. "Whoa!" Gabriel said in amazement. "What's going on?"

Then, the door swung open. The key popped out of the slot and fell on the floor. Gabriel stood motionless for a moment before taking two steps forward. Then he bent down to pick up the key. He put it into his pocket and stepped into the small room. Gabriel looked to his right and then to his left with his eyes. Nothing really stood out as very interesting. Maybe his adventure was a non-adventure after all. He continued into the room.

Finally, he saw something that did catch his eye. He walked closer to it. In the back of the room he saw a large sheet covering something that seemed to be taller than Gabriel. He guessed it to be at least six feet in height. "What is that?" Gabriel wondered as he hesitantly walked closer and closer. The floors seemed to groan with each step he made. No matter how quietly he walked, the floor seemed to fill the room with noise.

As Gabriel neared the item, he reached out. He was afraid to get too close to the foreign object that was covered by the sheet. When he reached out, the sheet fell to the floor instantly. Gabriel began to cough from a cloud of dust when the sheet hit the floor. As the dust cleared, he gasped at what he saw! It was a beautiful oil canvas painting that greeted him. The painting contained several items: a huge pirate ship was the first thing he saw. On the beautiful body of water, he spotted mermaids, each one beautiful in their own way. Gabriel had to admit it was the prettiest ocean. The color was what could only be described as perfectly blue-green in color. On a long boardwalk that connected the mainland to the ocean, he saw a frog with a crown. The frog was bigger than any frog he'd ever seen. He was smiling, too! "That's weird," Gabriel laughed.

Gabriel continued to look at the painting. He saw a tall man who looked to be over a hundred years old. He was pale with leathery skin. He also wore a robe that sparkled.

Next to him was another man who was shorter than the first, and he appeared to be full of energy. His eyes twinkled. He was wearing a multi-colored robe. Gabriel then spotted a young couple in the middle of a group. The man was holding the woman's hand. He wore a robe like the other two men. The woman was in a beautiful, long, and purple dress surrounded by a diverse group of people and animals. Everyone looked happy and full of smiles. Gabriel never knew animals could smile.

The couple was what he found most amazing from all the other creatures and people in the painting. The couple had fair skin and pale, blue eyes. The man had blond hair as well. "T-t-t-they look like me," Gabriel stuttered. He felt an instant connection to the unknown couple. He felt comforted by their smiles.

The painting was so life-like. It was obvious that the artist really made sure to take a lot of time to work on the painting to add as much detail as possible. Gabriel continued to study the couple in the middle. He couldn't get over how much they favored him.

Gabriel reached his fingers out to touch the couple. When he did, he felt his fingers not touch the painting but slide through it! "What just happened?" Gabriel yelped as he withdrew his hand quickly. The painting responded from this motion, and he watched a ripple of waves run through it, like when you toss a stone across a pond.

"Maybe I'm just seeing things!" Gabriel laughed and stepped even closer to the painting. He looked at the couple and then looked at the large frog. Suddenly, an idea came to Gabriel.

"I wonder..." Gabriel pondered his idea for a moment more. He touched the water and his hand went all the way through until he pulled it out again. Wildly, his heart began to beat inside his chest. Gabriel smiled, and then knew what he had to do. He rubbed his hands together as he began to stick both hands inside. His excitement was short lived, however.

"What are you doing?" he heard behind him as he slowly spun around.

Almost as quickly as it began, Gabriel's adventure was now over. Behind him, stood Gus, his cousin. Gabriel didn't speak immediately out of fear.

"I asked you a question, Pea Brain," Gus said as he folded his arms over his chest, looking like he was ready to punch Gabriel. The two exchanged looks and both were afraid to blink.

Gabriel stood there with his legs planted firmly onto the floor. He looked over his shoulder and stared back at the painting. Then he turned his attention back at Gus. He didn't know what to say.

He made a foolish choice and uttered, "Why aren't you at school?" Gabriel finally asked, throwing a question back at his cousin.

Gus snapped back, "Do you really think Mom is going to care I'm cutting school when she finds out you're in here? You're not supposed to be anywhere but your room!"

Gus never liked Gabriel. He never liked that Gabriel was different than the rest of the family. He never liked that even without an education he was smarter than Gus. He had to make sure he got Gabriel in big trouble. Maybe he could get him thrown out of the house for good. Gus snickered to himself as he approached his cousin. This could be his only chance to make his cousin sweat.

"Don't worry, Gabriel. I'm not going to hurt you. But I am going to tell and you're going to get in big trouble!" Gus smiled and winked playfully at Gabriel.

Gabriel walked toward Gus to try and talk this out. He held up his hands in an act of surrender. He bit the inside of his mouth, feeling his body dripping with sweat. His aunt and uncle never struck him, but he felt that day ended after this act of foolishness. He'd disobeyed their orders and would now have to pay. He suddenly felt his heart beat faster and faster as he stared back at his cousin and sighed. Gus approached him, backing Gabriel closer and closer to the painting once again.

Gabriel croaked out nervously, "Please, you can't tell..."

But Gabriel never got his words out because as Gus backed him closer and closer toward the painting, he pushed Gabriel's whole body into the painting and watched as Gabriel vanished into thin air!

CHAPTER SIX

Unfamiliar Place

Gabriel clutched his chest as he screamed and hollered. He soared through the air but was quickly falling closer to the ground below. He felt like he was falling from an airplane without a parachute. He closed his eyes, knowing the end was near. That was, until, he suddenly fell into a large pile of autumn leaves. Gabriel emerged from the pile almost immediately. He picked himself up and stood up again. He felt dizzy from the fall. "What happened?" Gabriel asked and looked around. The colors around him were like out of a greeting card showcasing the best of the autumn season. "That's weird. It's spring time."

As Gabriel wiped leaves from his body, he continued to survey his surroundings. None of what he saw looked familiar. Of course, he'd never been outside before. He felt very chilly and folded his arms across his chest to warm his body. He spotted an ocean with a long boardwalk connected to the mainland. There was a beautiful, natural forest around him. It really was a beautiful place, wherever he was. He felt a sense of peace.

That sense of peace was soon diminished when Gabriel heard the sounds of rustling trees and leaves crunching beneath what he assumed to be feet. The sounds of something moving through the forest behind him grew louder and louder. He suddenly became quite scared.

"Who's there?" Gabriel croaked out. He turned around and looked to find no one there. Gabriel assumed he must have been dreaming, as he still didn't recognize anything he saw. He then heard the loud rustling from the forest again. When he turned around this time, he saw a short man with a multi-colored robe on his body. He instantly recognized the man from the painting.

The man was humming to himself. It was a tune Gabriel did not recognize. The man was quite energetic as he kept walking. He did not see Gabriel at first. The only choice Gabriel had was to follow the man.

"Excuse me," he called to the man, weakly. "Excuse me!" Gabriel said a bit louder. "Excuse me!" This time, Gabriel shouted at the man.

Finally, the man turned around. "What? What do you need, young man? What?" The man looked irritated, as if Gabriel had interrupted his day. He stared at the young boy for a long time, waiting for an answer.

Gabriel replied weakly, "I'm sorry. But I seem to have ended up here out of nowhere. I need to find out how to get home."

The short man just threw up his hand. "I don't have time for games right now! Can't you see I'm busy? I must be getting home. My friend needs me, and then we have a meeting with The King! Good day!" He turned and walked away.

Gabriel pleaded with the man, "Please, sir..."

The short man cut him off. "No, no, I don't have the time. Try asking one of the owls. They're very wise, you know?" He snickered at his own joke and continued to hum his song from earlier.

Gabriel knew immediately the man didn't want to speak to him with such a silly suggestion. "An owl?" Gabriel snorted. "Oh, I get it. A *wise* owl."

The short man turned around again. He raised his eyebrow, "You're not from around here, are you?"

Gabriel shook his head, "No. I am not. Please help."

The short man turned again to walk away.

By this time, Gabriel was visibly upset. He was in a strange land and surrounded by strange, unfamiliar things. It wasn't long before Gabriel began to cry. "I understand," he said through his tears, and suddenly the short man turned around, yet another time.

For a moment, the short man thought he was losing his mind. Then, he heard the boy crying again. "Wait a minute! I recognize those tears." He moved closer to the young boy. "Gabriel?" The short man looked at him as he studied his face. "But it can't be, can it?"

Gabriel wiped his face with his sleeve. "How did you know my name?"

The short man stood toe-to-toe with Gabriel. The two were the same height. "It is you, Gabriel!" He laughed and kissed the boy's forehead. And suddenly, just as they had done twelve years ago, Gabriel's tears ceased. "Gabriel! You're home!"

"I'm home?" Gabriel replied. He shook his head. This man was crazy!

"Yes," the short man said after wiping his own tears away. "And it couldn't be better timed. We need your help!"

Gabriel didn't know what to say to that foolish request. "Wait! Who needs my help? What are you talking about? Who are you?"

"So many questions, young lad. Allow me to introduce myself. Gabriel, I'm your godfather, Abram."

Gabriel stood, perplexed by the man's words. He was even more confused than ever now.

"I don't have a godfather. I don't even have parents."

The short man jumped up in the air, excitedly. "But you do, Gabriel! You do!" Abram replied. "Oh, how long we've waited for your return!"

"My return?" Gabriel asked. His questions went unanswered.

"Follow me," Abram smiled, and motioned for Gabriel to follow, who wasn't sure what to do. However, seeing how he was still convinced this was all a dream, Gabriel didn't see the harm. Without asking further questions, he shrugged his shoulders and followed the short man. Down the path they went, deeper, and deeper into this strange, unknown land.

CHAPTER SEVEN

A Mermaid

Gabriel walked and walked and walked for what seemed like forever, but it never seemed to bother the short man in front of him. Abram did a lot of talking and kept saying that Gabriel had come at just the right time, but never would say why. Gabriel didn't try to question why, however.

Finally, the two reached another beautiful ocean. Gabriel recognized it, too, from the painting back in Harmony. The ocean was blue and green in color and he could feel the wind blow in his face from its waves. The water was absolutely perfect and seemed free of pollutants. As the two walked along a long boardwalk, you could see the bottom of the ocean. Ocean life of every possible color swam in the waters. It was a beautiful sight! Gabriel, who had been pretty silent during their long journey spoke again as they walked down it.

"What are we doing here?" Gabriel asked. "What is this place?"

Abram held a finger to his lips. "Hang on! We have to wait!"

"On what?" Gabriel asked. He was visibly impatient by his tone of voice

Abram hushed him again. "Quiet, Gabriel."

The two stared at the water from the end of the boardwalk. After what seemed like forever but was only a few minutes, a beautiful mermaid jumped into the air and then dove back into the water.

Abram once again laughed a contagious laugh. "Did you see that?" He asked pointing to the water. "She's here!"

Gabriel backed up, scared by what he just saw, wringing out the bottom of his now soaked shirt. "Whoa! What was that? A shark?"

Abram shook his head. "No, my boy! It was one of our beautiful mermaids! But it wasn't just *any* mermaid! Wait for it!" After about another thirty seconds, Gabriel looked into the water, and he saw just below the surface the same female creature rise above and her tail splash water, covering Gabriel and Abram.

"Hey!" Gabriel screamed. He wringed out his shirt a second time. "Watch it!"

Abram laughed again. "Fern, hello there! This is Gabriel. He's come back!"

Fern stared back at Gabriel and looked over at Abram. "You don't mean, *the* Gabriel? The one who is destined to save us?"

Abram nodded. "Yes, Fern! *That* Gabriel. He's the son of…"

Fern interrupted and smiled at Gabriel. She gave a nervous chuckle as she looked over him.

Gabriel just sighed and tapped his foot. "Will someone please explain to me what is going on?"

Abram and Fern exchanged looks.

"All in good time, Gabriel. You will learn everything all in good time. However, what I can tell you at this moment is Fern is my daughter. Isn't she beautiful?"

Fern laughed softly. "Oh, Daddy. You're embarrassing me."

Gabriel was confused. How could a mermaid be real? How could her father be a human? None of this made any sense! Abram broke Gabriel's thoughts and spoke excitedly to his daughter.

"What's the matter? Have you got a little crush on Gabriel here?" Abram teased Fern.

Gabriel had never thought about girls much before as he had only seen them on television. He had to admit, however, that Fern was the prettiest girl he had ever seen in real life. She had beautiful red hair and her eyes seemed to twinkle from the sunlight. He looked away as he didn't want to be guilty of staring at her. His cheeks filled with a red hue. He was caught staring.

"It's very nice to meet you," he finally said after a long, awkward silence. He cleared his throat.

"It's nice to meet you, too, Gabriel," Fern said. She pushed her wet, red hair back, nervously with her hand.

Abram stared at the two oblivious love birds. He then jumped high into the air, throwing his fists up as if he were cheering. "Oh, my goodness! I can't wait for Walter to see you again."

Fern smiled at Gabriel, who still looked confused in his face. The two watched as Abram put his hands together and rubbed them quickly as if he were cold, but then he began to close his eyes and whisper silently.

Gabriel was about to check on him. He was worried the man may be hurt. Then, as he approached him, he realized, based on Fern's shaking of her head, that he was not to be disturbed at the moment. "He's fine," Fern whispered. "Just wait," she continued.

There was that word again: *wait* . He was getting tired of waiting.

Abram then started jumping in the air again. "Walter, he's here! He's arrived! He's arrived!" He opened his eyes and smiled at Gabriel. "Message received. He should be here soon."

"Who should be here soon?" Gabriel asked, once again very confused.

"Well, Walter of course," Abram laughed. "The one who accompanied me when we brought you to your aunt and uncle's house. I just sent him a message."

"Back home, people just use phones for that sort of thing," Gabriel said, rolling his eyes.

Fern and Abram didn't seem amused by the joke.

Suddenly, a bright yellow and orange flash occurred and an older man, who looked to be at least a hundred years old, probably older, appeared. He was wearing a robe that appeared to sparkle when light hit it. He was much taller than the shorter man. It was silent as the old man stared at Gabriel for a long time. Then he finally spoke, "Gabriel, welcome home!"

Gabriel stood back as the man's voice was soft but booming. "Who are you?"

"I am Walter. I am your caretaker."

"My what?" Gabriel asked with an eyebrow raised.

Walter could tell he was scaring the boy. He took a moment to formulate his words with less intensity. "Gabriel, my boy, do not be afraid. I come bringing you good news." He held out his hands in a peace offering. "I helped take care of you during the first few months of your life. I know you must have a lot of questions, but it's not up to us to answer them. We have to take you to see The King first."

"The King?" Gabriel asked.

The two men nodded. "He'll explain everything, Gabriel." Suddenly, the beautiful mermaid swam away, leaving Gabriel alone with two strangers claiming to know so much about him.

"Again, will someone please explain what is going on?" Gabriel groaned. He suddenly felt quite annoyed.

CHAPTER EIGHT

The King

Walter and Abram again motioned for Gabriel to follow them. They gave no answer to Gabriel's burning questions. They took him deeper and deeper into the strange land. Gabriel felt safe with the two men and listened to the two talk. He suddenly stopped them as they continued along the paths.

"I'm sorry. I can't continue until I know a few things."

Walter smiled at Abram. "Well, we have a long journey ahead. Keep walking and I'll answer. Fair enough?"

Gabriel nodded and began his questions, "So, where are we? I, mean, what's the name of this place? How did I get here?"

The two men continued walking. Gabriel was amazed at their energy. They never seemed tired. They turned to one another and then looked at Gabriel. Abram spoke first, "You mean your aunt and uncle never told you anything about your parents or this place at all?"

Gabriel shook his head, "No. They never told me anything about any of this at all. I wasn't allowed to leave the house."

Walter took control before Abram could continue. "I'll take it from here, Abram." He sighed softly and finally answered his question, "This place is called The Land of Fenton. We are ruled under The Great King Shamus."

"It's beautiful," Gabriel said with a nod, looking at the natural resources around him.

"It is," Abram said with a smile. "It's a place where everyone is loved." He looked at Gabriel and said again, "Everyone, Gabriel."

"But you said there was trouble." Gabriel tilted his head. "How can a place so beautiful where everyone is loved be troubled?"

Walter tilted his head. "It appears not everyone shares our ideals in keeping this place beautiful. We have a great form of government, and our King is fair to all here. Yet, there are some out there who don't agree. These individuals, pirates, let's call them, wish to overthrow King Shamus."

Abram jumped in with an animated fashion, "They are led by a horrible captain. He rules with the intention of killing our King, and only you can make sure that doesn't happen!"

"What? How? No way! I'm just a kid!" Gabriel protested while shaking his head. "What can I do?"

Suddenly, almost out of nowhere, a voice spoke behind Gabriel. "You can do anything. You are part of a family with great power."

Gabriel turned around and spotted a frog sitting on a boulder. The frog was wearing a large crown. He watched in amazement as the older man and shorter man knelt before the frog.

"King Shamus, hello, sir!" Abram and Walter said in unison.

Gabriel remained standing. "Wait. You mean, you're King Shamus?"

The frog nodded and motioned for the two men to rise. "Yes, I am, Gabriel."

Gabriel remained polite but felt a little funny seeing a frog with a crown on his head, especially a frog who could speak. "Um, pleased to meet you, sir."

The King laughed and asked Gabriel to approach him. "I am well aware of your uncertainty based on the tone in your voice. However, it is very nice to meet you as well."

"Thank you, sir," Gabriel said with a smile. "I was told that after meeting you, I could be told in detail why it is so important I am here."

The King paused for a long time. He stared at Gabriel and then looked at Abram and Walter. "Do you think he's ready to hear the whole story, men?"

Walter and Abram nodded.

"Alright then. You want to hear the whole story? I guess like most stories, it's best to start at the beginning..."

CHAPTER NINE

The Story

Matthew and Eden Mason were the proud parents of a beautiful baby boy named Gabriel. Eden knew her wonderful baby boy would be destined for great things. She never let the blessing go to her head, however. She expressed her gratitude daily.

Eden and her sister Marge, like most in The Land of Fenton, were able to perform magic. In order to ensure pure magic was used, all those capable of magic were given guides and advisors throughout their training. Eden and Marge were taught by their father, Gabriel, that magic was only to be used for good. This was because everyone in The Land of Fenton wanted to make their home a beautiful place for everyone to enjoy, including animals.

Unfortunately, only one sister listened to the teachings of their father. Eden began at a young age to use her magic to help others. She helped animals in the forest learn to speak. She believed this to be her gift. However, Marge didn't like animals learning to speak, and so she cast spells on them reversing the spell, and as a result, made them unable to speak again. This spell was unable to be changed back. It was a powerful, yet dangerous spell.

Their father didn't like this and would tell Marge if she didn't behave, she would be banished from The Land of Fenton and sent to Harmony. Eden hated this fact, but her father assured her that Marge would be given plenty of chances to redeem her actions. He told her a story of a Creator who believed in forgiveness. He explained that some people choose evil over good and he still hoped Marge would find her way.

"None of us are perfect, Eden," Gabriel reminded his daughter. "We choose our own path in life. We must be willing to forgive."

Marge continued her mischief and didn't understand or care that her actions had consequences. King Shamus was watching everything that happened in his land. He was quite displeased.

Eden and Marge attended school together at Fenton Academy. They continued to learn all types of magic. While Eden continued to learn how to use her magic for good, Marge continued to quietly use her magic to defy authority.

While in school, Eden was very popular and made lots of friends, but Marge kept to herself, preferring to study the darker sides of magic. She did, however, open up to one person. She met one man she felt she could manipulate, and the two were inseparable. It was around this time that Marge's eyes turned from blue to a terrifying brown. Marge and her new boyfriend, Mort vowed together to take down The King and all of The Land of Fenton. Mort Canton shared his girlfriend's view that magic should have no consequence and decided to join her in the quest to conquer The Land of Fenton. This would be their downfall.

Eden met Matthew Mason when she was twenty years old at a graduation for those with magical powers. She was instantly attracted to his beautiful blond hair. Those with blond hair were considered to have a strong level of magical power. The two married six months later.

It wasn't long before Marge decided to never use her powers for good, even if it meant being banished from The Land of Fenton. In doing so, she no longer quietly practiced her abuse of magic, either. She antagonized her sister and father greatly. She would cast spells on the citizens of The Land of Fenton and caused all kinds of despair. She and Mort would stir up trouble whenever possible. Marge was tired of living in her sister's shadows. While Marge's father still loved his troubled daughter very much, her actions displeased him.

As time continued, and his daughter continued to spiral more and more out of control, the father was pushed into a state of depression. He was admitted to a recovery center, but he never, well, recovered. He later died of a broken heart after realizing his daughter would never change. After learning of her indirect involvement in her father's death, Marge and Mort were banished from The Land of Fenton.

It wasn't easy, but in an effort to move on with their lives, and to try to honor his memory, Eden and Matthew had a baby boy. They named him, Gabriel, after Eden's father.

For a little while, the family's happiness continued. They lived without fear of Marge or her new husband, Mort returning. They knew that if King Shamus ever knew of her return, she would be locked up for her previous crimes. Although banished from The Land of Fenton, some found their way back. These pirates kept watchful eyes over the land, waiting for a moment to take over the place that shut them out.

Sadly, just when things were looking up for Eden and Matthew, tragedy happened again. Three months after Gabriel's birth, A gang of pirates known as The Dagger-Baggers captured Matthew and Eden. They took them far, far away.

CHAPTER TEN

The Dagger-Baggers

The King looked at Gabriel after he finished his story and wiped a tear away. He was obviously still grieving after all these years later.

Gabriel wiped a tear from his eyes, too. "Are they dead?" Gabriel asked. "What happened to them?"

"There are people who believe they are dead, I'm afraid," The King replied. "But there are others who have sworn they have seen them." He gave a quick look to Abram, but it went unnoticed to Walter and Gabriel.

"I'd like to believe they are still alive," Gabriel sniffled.

The King nodded, sympathetically, "Me too."

Gabriel stared at King Shamus for a long time before asking, "I still don't understand why you need me now. What can I do?"

"The Dagger-Baggers are back! They are threatening to overtake my throne! If they take my throne, then all of us in The Land of Fenton will be at risk. You are the only being left with pure magic. Remember, you have blond hair," The King replied, almost pleading in tone.

Gabriel shook his head, "I don't know how to do any magic. How can I have any pure magic?"

Walter and Abram approached Gabriel and each gently touched one of his shoulders, "That's why we're here," said Abram.

"We will teach you," continued Walter.

Gabriel sighed heavily, "But what if I fail?"

King Shamus shook his head, "That won't happen. The Dagger-Baggers are the hardest, toughest, and fiercest pirates in the land, but you have something they don't, my boy."

"What's that?" Gabriel asked, tilting his head to the side.

"Well," King Shamus, began, but took a moment to eat a fly that flew high above his head. He then smiled. "Sorry about that. Anyway, you have love in your heart. You have to trust your heart's instincts. Follow it, Gabriel. If you can believe in yourself, we will arm you with the best soldiers to see that you win. This is your purpose in life!"

"But…" Gabriel started to ask but watched as suddenly, The King vanished. "Wait! Come back," Gabriel pleaded.

"It's okay," Walter patted Gabriel's back to comfort him. "He'll be back."

Gabriel turned to Abram, "What are the Dagger-Baggers like?"

Abram explained, "The Dagger-Baggers are made up of pirates, bandits, who have been banished from The Land of Fenton. They use their magic for evil. But because they have been banished, their magic is weak. Together, however, they can make horrible things happen."

"Like what?" Gabriel asked.

Walter stepped in, "You've heard of hurricanes, right?"

"Yes, of course," nodded Gabriel.

Walter continued, "That's all the doing of the Dagger-Baggers and their magic. They are the designers of all the hurricanes and storms on the seas. They also create other things, like earthquakes. Together, the Dagger-Baggers are powerful force. Captain N.H. is their supreme leader. He strived to create his own Kingdom that he thought would be a perfect alternative to our own."

"You mean…?" Gabriel asked but didn't finish the question.

Walter nodded, "Exactly. He's from Harmony. He was one of the first beings banished from The Land of Fenton, many, many, many years ago."

"And the Captain wants to be the new king," Gabriel said, finally putting the pieces together.

"Precisely," said Abram.

"Captain N.H. is very powerful and has armed himself with very powerful pirates, including one very loyal servant. No one knows who the servant is, however, as like all the other pirates, the servant wears a mask," explained Walter.

"I wonder why that is," Gabriel pondered.

"The servant is probably hiding a deep, dark secret," said Abram.

"Or the servant is merely just an ugly being," laughed Walter.

Abram looked at his friend and teased, "Oh, now who is the smart-aleck?"

Walter hung his head in shame, "I know. I know. Sometimes it slips out when I think about how evil Captain N.H. can be to others."

"But for now, your training begins," Abram reminded Gabriel.

"No. Now, OUR training begins," Gabriel corrected him.

Walter and Abram exchanged smiles.

CHAPTER ELEVEN

Gabriel's First Birthday

Over the next several months, Gabriel trained every day with Walter and Abram. He learned spells from Abram and martial arts that would help him in combat for battles from Walter. Abram was known for his skills in magic. He once taught at Fenton Academy. Walter was a known to many as a mighty warrior.

Gabriel learned spells that would teach him how to fight against the pirates, particularly against the servant and Captain N.H. He also learned the spell of how to teach animals to speak, like his mother. As each day passed, he grew stronger and stronger and more knowledgeable in his knowledge of magic. He was warned, however, that magic must only be used for good, and never for evil acts.

One morning, while doing spells, Gabriel was asked by Abram, "You know what tomorrow is, don't you?"

Gabriel turned his head to the side and replied, "I don't think so. Should I?"

Abram sighed, "Boy, your aunt and uncle really were monsters, weren't they?"

Gabriel smiled before replying, "I don't think I should answer that. Aren't there monsters in The Land of Fenton that are friendly?"

As it was now winter, Walter was busy gathering wood for a fire. He smiled, "See, Abram! I told you he had the heart of his grandfather and father."

Abram continued where he left off, "Gabriel, tomorrow is your thirteenth birthday!"

Gabriel looked at him, shocked, almost confused. "My birthday?"

Walter walked over, carrying the large handful of kindling and spoke gently, "Abram, be nice to the boy. He's never celebrated his birthday before. Not to worry, Gabriel. We are going to change that. We are also having a party in your honor. We are having it here in the backyard."

Gabriel suddenly felt his heart beat faster with excitement, "You mean a birthday party for me? Really?"

Abram smiled and nodded, "Just for you, my boy."

The young boy couldn't believe what he was hearing and jumped up and down. He suddenly stopped soon after. He had a terrible thought, "Are you sure it's safe? What if the Dagger-Baggers find out?"

Walter shook his head and started back for the small cottage, "Just leave that to us, okay?"

Abram pressed the matter a little further, "But you must promise us you will work hard tonight and tomorrow morning on all your training!"

Gabriel nodded, "Yes! Yes, of course I will!"

The two men laughed, and Gabriel immediately resumed work on his training.

In the far distance, through a large telescope, a pair of eyes looked on at the scene and a shrill scream rang out. Others around, quickly scattered out of fear.

"I can't believe it! They are having a birthday party for him now! Someone better stop this from happening. Birthdays should not be a celebration! Is that clear?" The voice was booming and made the ground shake, causing a small, but brief earthquake.

The pirates looked on at their supreme leader. He was a short man with a round belly. He pulled away from the telescope. He scratched at the hair on his head, which seemed to move. It was an obvious hairpiece. With fear in their eyes, no one answered. They wanted to respect his wishes, but they knew how difficult defeating a being like Gabriel would be for anyone who tried.

One of the pirates spoke up nervously, "But, sir, he's stronger than we think!"

Captain N.H. continued, unfazed, "I don't want any excuses that he got away or you couldn't find him! He's having his birthday party tomorrow, and you will find him. You will make him suffer. Have I made myself clear?"

A voice from the darkness suddenly spoke from underneath a mask, "Yes, Captain, our master, it's crystal clear!"

The other pirates nodded in agreement.

"Very good, my humble servant," Captain N.H. smiled and looked back on the scene at Gabriel.

The Captain began to laugh, wickedly. "Tomorrow is your birthday, but it won't be a happy one. It will be a terrible one."

Soon, all the pirates joined in laughing at the planned takedown of Gabriel. The Captain had more plans, too.

CHAPTER TWELVE

Unwelcome Guests

Shortly after Gabriel's training the following morning, Walter and Abram began hanging decorations outside. Gabriel saw birthday parties on television a few times, but he'd never seen decorations like this before. The decorations in The Land of Fenton were vastly different.

For starters, Walter and Abram used jars and fireflies for natural light outside, which Walter said would look beautiful once the sun went down and the guests arrived. He also added streamers, but these weren't made like traditional, paper streamers. These streamers were made out of fall leaves of the most beautiful colors. Every time Gabriel tried to help, Walter shooed him back into the cottage.

Abram reminded him, "It's your birthday, my boy! Go back inside!"

Walter nodded, "We know you're eager!" He laughed softly. "Just wait!"

Gabriel tried to focus his energy on anything else to occupy his time. He sat in the cottage's small living room area and studied from his spell book. There were so many spells, but all were positive in nature. He then focused on reading from the big book. Walter often told Gabriel about it. The book was filled with stories of a loving Creator. "This is wonderful! I have so much to learn!" Gabriel told himself as he flipped through the big book.

Gabriel was interrupted from his studies by Walter walking into the room. "It's time, Gabriel." He smiled, and Abram stood behind him with a big, almost dopey grin on his face.

"Come outside! Come outside!" Abram chanted over and over.

Gabriel grinned and followed his godfather and caretaker outside. He couldn't believe what he saw. The two men went all out, and every sight was breathtaking for Gabriel. "All of this for me?" He asked. He continued to look and saw a small stage. Hanging above the stage were the streamers and a banner that said, "Happy birthday, Gabriel" in big, block letters. It was beginning to grow dark outside and the firefly-filled jars gave a beautiful, natural glow.

"Don't worry," Abram insisted, "They can breathe in there. We can release them after the party!"

Before he could take in much more, the guests began to arrive. They were characters you'd only see in books. Some were lions and bears, and others were owls, geese, rabbits, and beavers. He saw dragons, otters, and birds of every color imaginable. Truly, every type of animal one could imagine, somehow found their way to Gabriel's birthday. There were humans, too, but they were definitely in the minority. What amazed Gabriel most was that all the animals in attendance could speak! Gabriel was amazed, and for the first time in his life, he felt like he was among friends. Each guest greeted Gabriel and handed him a gift.

Walter pointed out a few of the animals who were there to play music. "Ever heard of the band, 'Basket of Kittens?'"

Gabriel shook his head, "Not until tonight." He smiled as he watched the kittens begin to play instruments. Gabriel stared in amazement, "How is this even possible?" He felt like it was all a dream.

The final guest to arrive came in a carriage, and everyone began to kneel, so Gabriel followed suit. He wouldn't make the same mistake twice. He knew who this guest was.

"His Majesty," Gabriel said, greeting King Shamus.

King Shamus smiled when he exited the carriage. "Now, now, Gabriel! Please, as you were. Happy birthday, my boy."

"Thank you, sir," Gabriel replied. "I'm happier you're here."

The guests rose to their feet, and King Shamus hopped along the backyard with Gabriel. "I am glad to be here, too. I have some news to share with you."

Gabriel enjoyed being around The King as he felt he was one of the best connections he had to his parents, "Oh? You do?"

The King nodded proudly, "Yes. It's something I need to tell you about your father."

Gabriel tilted his head, confused, "Why didn't you tell me before?"

"It wasn't the right time. I had to ensure you were ready," The King said softly.

More confused than ever, Gabriel replied, "Ready? Ready for what, sir?"

"For battle." The King said, "And now that you're nearing the end of your training, I think it's time you knew."

"Well, what is it?" Gabriel asked.

The King smiled and looked up at Gabriel. He cleared his throat. "Well..."

Before The King could continue, a loud rustling noise was heard in the distance. Horses neighed and galloped into the fields. Gabriel and the rest of the guests could hear whips being slapped against their bodies.

"What's going on?" The King uttered, making a loud croak.

"I'm not sure," Gabriel said, his own voice shaking. The noises grew louder and louder as they approached.

Near the party scene, glass jars containing the fireflies, started falling one by one, smashing to the ground below. The smaller party guests, mostly animals, started scurrying away in different directions.

"Run home! Run home!" one of them screamed, "It's the Captain!"

At that moment, King Shamus appeared on a majestic white horse.

King Shamus began to hop quickly in another direction. "Oh, no," The King croaked again, "They've found us! I don't know how, but they've found us!"

The King began to hop as fast as he could, and suddenly his crown fell off his head as he began to hop.

"Wait, wait! King Shamus, stop!" Gabriel cried, chasing after him.

"Don't worry about me! Save yourself, Gabriel!" The King cried out.

Gabriel looked on with panic as the uninvited guests invaded and tore through his birthday party scene. He saw guests run away. Some, however, weren't as lucky. The pirates tore through. They captured many of the smaller creatures and locked them in cages.

One duck screamed, "Help me!" He then began losing the ability to speak and suddenly screeched out a familiar sound a duck makes. "Quuuaaaaccckkk!"

Gabriel watched in horror as the pirate's spell took effect. The pirate snickered, "Ain't so smart without lips, is you?"

"Oh, my goodness," Gabriel started to run, feeling defenseless, almost instantly forgetting his training.

The pirates began to throw torches into the cottage, burning it to the ground. Gabriel ran and ran, looking around for anyone he could find, "Walter! Abram!"

"Over here, my boy," came a weak reply, and Gabriel saw Walter lift his hand as he laid on the ground. He was alive, but he looked badly wounded.

Gabriel rushed to his side, "Walter!"

"I'm okay, Gabriel!" Walter assured him, "Just knocked down is all. Maybe a bit bruised." The two could hear the pirates' screams of combat around them, and the screams of the defenseless party guests. "Gabriel, you need to find The King!"

"What about you?" Gabriel asked, shaking his head. "Where's Abram?"

Walter shook his head, "I'm fine! You must find King Shamus!"

Gabriel helped Walter to his feet and Walter slowly spoke again after coughing, "I haven't found Abram yet. But I will!"

Gabriel nodded and took off running to search for King Shamus. The smoke from the cottage was rising, and he knew the home was near collapse. "King Shamus! Where are you?"

He searched and searched and continued calling out The King's name. The fields and forests were covered with smoke and fire, but there was no sign of The Land of Fenton's beloved frog. When it seemed all hope was lost, he suddenly heard a voice.

"Gabriel..."

From a distance Gabriel thought he heard someone try to say his name. He turned and took off toward the source of the sound. He called out loudly, "Speak!"

"Gabriel..." the voice cried out again. It was weaker this time.

Finally, he reached a large boulder. It was the same boulder Gabriel saw months before. He collapsed on his knees and saw a badly wounded, heavily bloodied, King Shamus. "Oh, my goodness! You're hurt!"

The King coughed and was stretched out over the boulder. His feet twitched a bit and looked up at Gabriel. His crown was missing. "Gabriel, please. I have to tell you what I was going to tell you earlier."

Gabriel shook his head. "There will be time for that later. We have to get you some help!"

King Shamus shook his head, "I'm afraid there's no time to get help for me. Captain N.H. has won this time. But, Gabriel, you can and must find him." King Shamus coughed again.

Gabriel began to cry, "No! No! Please..." Gabriel couldn't finish.

King Shamus looked at Gabriel, "Let me explain to you while I can."

Gabriel nodded, tears flowing down his cheeks.

"Gabriel, Captain N.H. is my son, and he's your father's brother."

The young boy stared at him. "I thought my grandfather died."

King Shamus coughed again, his voice now barely above a whisper. "No, that was your mother's father."

Gabriel's eyes widened, "So, you're my grandfather?"

"Yes," King Shamus replied and coughed again, "There is evil in every family. But it's up to each member whether to follow the right path or not. Captain N.H., I'm afraid, like your Aunt Marge and Uncle Mort, followed the wrong path."

Gabriel stared at his dying grandfather. "I've got to stop Captain N.H. before it's too late!"

"Now do you see why we needed your help?" The King replied, weaker than ever. His eyes looked murky and his breaths quickened.

Gabriel nodded and replied, "But that means..." Before Gabriel could even finish, he heard one long breath taken and looked down to see King Shamus. He was dead.

"That means I'm the new king," a voice boomed from behind Gabriel. He turned around to see a short man with a round belly. Gabriel studied the man even further and saw on his head a familiar crown.

Gabriel, overcome with emotion, turned to the lifeless body of his grandfather, the former king and then back at Captain N.H., who was now laughing, wickedly, "Well, aren't you going to bow at my feet, Nephew?" He saw a flash of lightning in the distance, only amplifying Captain N.H.'s terrifying demeanor. He then galloped away on his white horse and vanished into the night.

CHAPTER THIRTEEN

Prince Gabriel

Gabriel stared at his grandfather's lifeless body, overcome with emotion. The lightning struck again. The rains, however, never came. Suddenly, he heard a familiar voice calling out.

"Gabriel! Come quickly," screamed the voice.

Gabriel took off running toward the voice to find Abram standing near the burned-out cottage that Gabriel considered his home.

"Our home! Our beautiful home," Abram cried out.

"It's okay, it's okay," Walter replied. "We should be glad to be alive. A home can be replaced!"

The two men gathered up debris left behind by the pirates. For a moment, Gabriel was motionless. Many of his presents were either burned or smashed to hundreds of pieces.

"Did you find The King?" Walter asked while he continued picking up debris.

Gabriel looked down at his feet again. His fists clenched. "I'm afraid he's not with us anymore," Gabriel replied.

"What? What do you mean?" Walter croaked, holding back tears of his own.

Abram covered his mouth, not wanting to hear the news as Gabriel explained the news and everything he learned. "Wow! I can't believe this! Everything he predicted. It came true!"

The two men knelt before him, and Gabriel shook his head.

"No, no, please! Stop! Don't! I sure don't feel like a prince. Besides, we still have to take the new king out. He's overthrown my grandfather!"

"We have to stop him," Walter hit his fist against his other hand.

Gabriel shook his head, "But how? You saw how quickly he took out the party guests!"

"We weren't prepared then," Abram snapped. "We'll be prepared next time!"

Walter quickly added, "And this time, we'll have our army!"

Abram and Walter took off into the forest with Gabriel leading the way. They walked for over an hour and each step seemed more difficult than the one before. The reason was because Gabriel and Walter were carrying a large, metal box.

"Are you sure this is the right way?" Abram asked, feeling as though they were walking in circles.

"Hush, Abram," Walter scolded him. "Trust the boy!"

Abram quickly nodded and after a few minutes, Gabriel stopped. "Here! This is the place. Stop."

Walter and Abram looked down, and each knelt after Walter and Gabriel carefully placed the large, metal box on the ground.

Below them was the lifeless body of the former king. Once a mighty warrior, who ruled over The Land of Fenton, Gabriel's grandfather was dead. He once ate flies, but now he was now being swarmed by them. Gabriel quickly shooed them away by casting a spell.

"I wish there was a spell to bring someone back to life," Gabriel said as he wiped a tear away from his eyes."

Walter nodded, and touched his shoulder.

Abram, who was carrying a shovel, began to dig a grave. He placed the body of King Shamus into the box. Each exchanged kind words about their king, ending with Gabriel.

"We won't let your death go unnoticed, Grandfather. We will defeat Captain N.H., his servant, and all the Dagger-Baggers."

Gabriel realized in that moment the Captain should probably be referred to as The King and mumbled out loud to no one in particular, "I refuse to call him King N.H. and furthermore, I will make sure the right person will take the throne!"

Walter interjected, "You realize who the true king is, right?"

Gabriel suddenly realized whom it was that Walter meant.

Gabriel protested, "I just meant the right person was out there. I didn't necessarily mean myself."

Walter grinned, "But that person is you!"

Gabriel shook his head, "Stepping onto our domain today and killing our king was a declaration of war as far as I'm concerned."

Walter and Abram nodded in agreement.

"So, I say we round up the best of our men and women and take down Captain N.H. and the Dagger-Baggers. Then, we can take back my Grandfather's throne," Gabriel said.

Gabriel sighed after a quick look at the mound of dirt covering King Shamus' coffin and then stuck out his hand in an effort to seal the deal. Walter placed his hand over Gabriel's and Abram placed his on the top.

"For my Grandfather," Gabriel said confidently.

"For King Shamus," Abram said.

"For the Land of Fenton," Walter said with a nod.

The three turned and walked back to the burned-out cottage.

CHAPTER FOURTEEN

Fern's Advice

The next several weeks Gabriel prepared for battle against Captain N.H. and the Dagger-Baggers. While he knew he was growing stronger and stronger with each lesson from Walter and Abram, he also became more and more anxious.

The cottage had long since been rebuilt, with a little help from Walter, Gabriel, and Abram's magic. Gabriel's training included learning to use a shield and sword properly. He was told that even his magic wouldn't help him win the fight. He had no intentions of winning with magic alone. He needed faith. Faith in himself and faith in the power of good over evil. He had to rely on the skills taught to him by Walter, a Warrior.

"I have taught you everything I know," Walter said one day. "Now it's up to you to believe in yourself!"

"I'm just worried I won't be ready to stand up to Captain N.H.," replied Gabriel.

Walter shook his head, "You won't defeat him if you hold on to that defeated attitude."

"Agreed," Abram added. "You need to have more confidence in your abilities. Why don't you take a walk to clear your head?"

Gabriel agreed and walked down the familiar path he and Abram took toward the ocean. He didn't expect to find anything there, but he walked down along the boardwalk. He looked up and saw the stars. Each one was so very bright. He felt he could touch them with his hands. As he looked down toward the water, he saw the same stars dancing along the water. The beautiful water lit up from the glow of the moon and stars. His trance of the beautiful night was soon ended, however.

"I didn't expect to see you out this way," whispered a voice behind Gabriel.

Gabriel turned but didn't see anyone on the boardwalk. "Who said that?" Gabriel asked.

A voice giggled sweetly, "Gabriel, it's me, silly! It's Fern!"

Suddenly, he felt a large splash of water hit him. "Hey! Quit it!" Gabriel yelped.

"Oh, come on," Fern laughed. "Don't be afraid! What are you doing out here, anyway?"

Gabriel just shrugged, "I don't know. I guess I'm anxious about tomorrow. We're preparing for battle to face off against Captain N.H., the servant, and all the pirates."

Fern stared back at Gabriel for a long time before speaking, "Being afraid will get you nowhere."

Gabriel protested, "But wouldn't you be afraid?"

Fern smiled, "Yes. But if I had a heart like yours, I would know I had nothing to worry about. Think of it like this, if you were back in Harmony what would you be doing right now?"

Gabriel pondered the question but could only come up with a one-word response, "Nothing."

"Exactly!" Fern said with a wink. "You've been given this amazing opportunity, this amazing adventure. You wouldn't have that back in Harmony. *Nothing* is pretty boring, Gabriel. *Something*, however, something is extremely exciting. Think about it."

Gabriel stared as the beautiful mermaid swam away. He watched her tail glow under the stars and the moonlight. "She's beautiful," Gabriel said out loud. He quickly regained control of his thoughts.

He had to admit Fern was right. He turned and walked down the boardwalk again, and back toward the cottage. He wasn't sure if he felt less uneasy about going into battle, however. He did, know for sure that his heart felt stronger than ever before.

CHAPTER FIFTEEN

Walter's Gift

Gabriel didn't sleep at all that night. Around 7 o'clock the next morning, a gentle knock came from his bedroom door.

"Come in, please," Gabriel called out.

Abram walked in and hesitated before approaching Gabriel's bedside. "Prince Gabriel, it's time."

Gabriel nodded. He slowly slid out of bed and stumbled toward his dresser and began to dress. Abram began explaining how the day would play out. They were to gather their men and women and enter the outlands of The Land of Fenton to face off against the evil Dagger-Baggers.

"There's one more thing, Prince Gabriel," Abram said gently.

Gabriel looked up at him after pulling on a pair of dark black combat boots. "Yes, what is it?"

"Walter has something he'd like to present to you when you are done eating breakfast."

Gabriel nodded and walked into the bathroom. He looked at himself in the mirror. He breathed in and out slowly.

"This is for my family," Gabriel said to his reflection. He suddenly felt a pain in his stomach so great he almost wished he could climb back in bed or, worse, he was back in his old, uncomfortable cot in Harmony.

Gabriel finished dressing and walked into the main room of the cottage and spotted Abram and Walter eating breakfast. Gabriel sat down to join them and sighed. "This could be my last breakfast," Gabriel uttered.

Walter scooped some eggs onto Gabriel's plate and shook his head, "Don't talk like that, please! You will win if you believe in yourself!"

Abram touched Gabriel's shoulder. "You must have faith, Gabriel."

Gabriel submitted and nodded his head. He still wasn't sure, however.

The three ate quietly and only spoke when absolutely necessary. Walter and Abram were well aware of Gabriel's nervousness but tried at all costs not to bring it up. They wanted the boy to believe in himself, but they knew there was no convincing him otherwise. It was out of their hands now.

After breakfast, Gabriel and Walter walked outside at his caretaker's insistence. "I have to give you something," he said.

Gabriel tilted his head, "What is it?"

"You will see," Walter smiled.

The two moved through the tall grass in the fields and into a small shed that was saved from the initial burning from the pirates. Inside, on a small workshop table, Walter lifted a large sheet and Gabriel was greeted by a beautiful handcrafted sword and shield.

"Oh, my goodness!" Gabriel cried, absolutely breathless.

"Gabriel, as your caretaker it is my responsibility to make sure you are cared for at all times," Walter began. "I made these items for you. Your training is now complete. Abram trained you in magic, and I trained you in your combat. We couldn't be more proud."

Walter lifted the sword. "Be careful with these things. Use them for good. I've watched you, Gabriel, these last months, and I must say I'm quite impressed. You have shown to me you have mighty skills, and you have strong courage as well. You are ready for this battle, Gabriel. You are!"

Gabriel stared back at Walter and nodded as he held the sword in his hand. Walter handed him the shield, and

Gabriel held it tightly in his other hand. "Thank you, Walter," Gabriel said with a confidence that he felt came out of nowhere.

"You can thank me when you're the new king," Walter replied.

Gabriel nodded confidently.

CHAPTER SIXTEEN

The Battle

Gabriel walked out of the small cottage workshop with his shield strapped to his back and sword tucked neatly behind it. He hugged Abram and Walter goodbye but promised he would be home soon.

On his way out, Abram began to tear up. Gabriel waved his hand over his head.

"I used to do the same thing to you when you were a baby," Abram pointed out as the tears left his face.

"I know. Walter told me," Gabriel said with a smile. "Your tears are not going to bring me home safely," Gabriel reminded him.

Abram nodded. "You are right. Now, go out there and win! We love you, Gabriel."

The two hugged again, and Gabriel headed down the path toward the outskirts of The Land of Fenton. He hummed the now familiar tune he heard Abram hum the day they met. "This is my story, this is my song…" Gabriel sang softly.

As he walked down the path, he saw many beautiful sights. There were mountains taller than any he heard about on television. He saw rivers, creeks, and lakes with no signs of harmful chemicals. The Land of Fenton was something to behold.

While on the path, Gabriel also spotted many animals. The ones who could speak voiced their support for Gabriel. Those who couldn't speak, took a moment to bow toward him. He really felt special when he saw those actions. It was humbling, too, given how his life began in Harmony.

A few days into his journey, he met up with his army. He was joined by men and women. Residents of The Land of Fenton, now soldiers, were ready and armed to take down

Captain N.H. and his evil pirates. It wasn't long before Gabriel's army grew to over one hundred men and women. Although he was only thirteen years old, he was the leader of men and women much older. They were looking to Gabriel for leadership. In his heart, he knew he was up for the challenge, but it was still rewarding to know people looked to him for guidance.

"We won't let you down, sir," one of the much older soldiers told Gabriel.

Often his soldiers would call him Prince Gabriel as they traveled, but Gabriel would insist they call him only by his first name. He said their mission was to overthrow the new and evil king. They were to get justice for the deceased King Shamus.

As they reached the outskirts of The Land of Fenton, none of the soldiers saw anything out of the ordinary. Gabriel turned to his left and then to his right. The soldiers circled Gabriel to protect him at all costs.

"Where are they?" Gabriel asked as he surveyed the surroundings.

Not far from Gabriel's army, Captain N.H., now also known as King N.H., but only to himself and his followers, looked on. He peered out through his telescope. He finally spoke up to his followers, "We will descend upon them soon, but for now, we will make them wait. We will lure them into a false sense of security."

"Great idea, Master," echoed the servant. "Should we send them a signal, so they know we see them?"

"Not yet. We'll wait until dawn when they aren't expecting it," Captain N.H. replied with another wicked laugh.

The servant then looked through a telescope, too. "Rest up tonight, Gabriel! You'll need it."

Gabriel and his soldiers decided to go ahead and set up camp after several hours of silence from Captain N.H.'s pirates. "I don't see any sign of them," Gabriel stated. "I think it's safe for us to begin setting up our camp."

The men and women began setting up their tents and put together fires. Meals were made as well. Gabriel knew something wasn't right, however. He knew his uncle, Captain N.H. was up to something.

"There's a plan here. I just don't know what," Gabriel said to one of his soldiers.

During dinner, the army enjoyed a small and jovial time as one unit. They sang songs in support of their loving Creator. They knew the celebration would be short lived, however. Each gave thanks and expressed a faith for protection over them.

Gabriel tried to sleep that night but sleep never came. He insisted on placing two guards outside of every tent to ensure there would be no surprise attacks during the night. As he tried to sleep, he thought about Walter and Abram. He could only hope they were safe, too. He tossed and turned in his tent, fighting for sleep. He was losing this battle, unfortunately.

Suddenly, just before daybreak, and in the distance, Gabriel heard a loud rustling sound. It was a sound he recognized from his birthday party.

"It's them!" Gabriel shouted from inside his tent. He was already dressed, and quickly grabbed his sword and shield and strapped them on. "Men, women, let's go," was Gabriel's order.

At that moment, all the tents were exited at once. Men and women of all size and power and prepared to fight the enemy, emerged from their tents. When the dust from the commotion of the pirate's entrance settled, Gabriel spotted the familiar white horse and his uncle wearing the crown.

"Hello, Nephew, we meet again," Captain N.H. smirked.

To his right was a soldier dressed in black with a mask on, similar to the other soldiers; only the lips could be seen.

"Master, shall I kill the boy?" the soldier asked, pulling out a sword.

Gabriel swallowed heavily in his throat after hearing those words, but he grabbed his sword from its sheath. "Let's do this!"

Captain N.H. grinned, but shook his head to his servant, "Now, now, my servant, is that the way you want to speak to your flesh and blood?"

Gabriel looked puzzled. With his sword lowered, he watched as the servant removed the mask. He looked back in horror at who he saw staring back at him. "No! It can't be!"

"Oh, but it can," the servant said, smiling.

"Aunt Marge?" Gabriel croaked out.

Aunt Marge nodded, "Did you miss me, Sweet Nephew?"

CHAPTER SEVENTEEN

The Trap

Gabriel stared at the brown eyes looking back at him. He didn't know what to think. Had she followed him through the oil canvas painting? How did she get here? Was she here the whole time? He had so many questions. "How...?" Gabriel managed to utter.

"How?" Aunt Marge replied. "You want to know how I ended up back here?"

Gabriel nodded, more terrified than ever at the woman who raised him but kept him prisoner for the first twelve years of his life.

"Let's just say, when I'd leave you alone every day, I wasn't exactly doing that just to be cruel. I was coming back here to learn more magic. I was banned from The Land of Fenton. For years, I blamed you and your mother for my unhappiness. But I eventually realized I could make my own happiness. I found a new way to reach the place that shut me out. So, with a little help from that silly painting and Captain N.H., 'the servant' was born." Marge waved her mask in triumphant victory.

Captain N.H. looked at Gabriel with a shake of his head, "You really believed that your aunt wouldn't find a way to bring you to me? She knew you'd come back here eventually."

"It was all part of our plan," Marge continued. "So, now with your training complete, we're going to kill you. Legend has it that if you kill a blond with strong power, the power automatically becomes yours upon their death. I think your power will do just fine, Nephew!" She pointed her sword at him and winked.

"You got the ending figured out yet, Gabriel?" Captain N.H. snickered, "You fell right into our trap. And once you're dead, and with all your magic, we can create the perfect Kingdom!"

It all made sense to Gabriel now. The key was left out for him to find. It wasn't by accident, after all. Aunt Marge lured him here on purpose. Gabriel picked up his sword and held it straight toward the sky, and it shined right into the face of his aunt. "And how do you know I won't try to kill both of you right now?" Gabriel asked.

"You couldn't hurt us if you tried," Marge pointed out.

"I just might. I've had a lot of training from Walter and Abram, and you just admitted I was a powerful being. I learned plenty from them," Gabriel snapped back. "I learned self-confidence, love, and more in just a few months with Walter and Abram than I ever learned with you and Uncle Mort."

"How dare you!" Marge screamed "I gave you a home. I gave you food!"

"That's not how I remember it!" Gabriel shot back, his eyes were fixed on his target.

"Since when did you get any kind of backbone," Marge laughed, calling Gabriel's bluff. "We both know you have the backbone of a jellyfish."

"I'm not scared of you any longer, Aunt Marge!" Gabriel said with confidence. His heart continued to beat in his chest with anticipation.

At that moment, he saw his aunt hit his sword with her own. "Well, Gabriel, let's see what you've learned!"

The two began to exchange blows with their swords, but never hitting one another directly. Marge began to mutter to herself and that's when Gabriel realized she was using magic to fight with him. He vowed to Walter and Abram to win by his warrior skills alone.

"I can do this! I have the heart. She doesn't have that," Gabriel told himself, trying to remember the words of Fern. He lunged at his aunt, but she continued to block every move he made. Gabriel was soon breathless. Other soldiers, from both sides, looked on at the scene. They were amazed at Gabriel's ability to keep up with his aunt, despite her use of magic.

"I can do this all day, Aunt Marge!" Gabriel said as he continued to cross swords with his cruel aunt.

Marge shook her head. "Please! Give up, Gabriel! It's over!" Marge laughed when suddenly she heard a loud noise from one of the animals.

Seizing the moment of her brief distraction, Gabriel, lunged forward and knocked his aunt's sword out of her hand. Marge fell to the ground. Gabriel then towered over her and pressed on her stomach, ready to drive the sword into her. Marge screamed in terror, begging to be let free. "That's not fair! I *hate* animals!"

Gabriel stared back at his aunt but said nothing.

"Please, no! I'm sorry, Gabriel. I should have been nicer to you," Marge looked up at him with growing fear in her dark eyes.

He didn't believe anything he was hearing. He was ready to finish her off so he could move on to his next prospect, the evil new king. He moved the sword closer, closer.

A voice behind the two rang out, "That's enough! Get off her now!"

Gabriel turned without letting his foot off Marge to see Walter. The young soldier stared at the tall, older gentleman looking at him, "Walter! What are you doing here?"

Walter's words were now soft and gentle, "She's not worth it. She can't fight without her magic. Gabriel, she's only submitting to the will of the wicked king. Remember, only you have the key to sending her back," he pointed out.

Suddenly, Walter's words made sense, and Gabriel withdrew his sword from being close to her body. "Go on, I'll deal with you later," he uttered. He watched his aunt scramble to her feet. She cowered behind Captain N.H., and together, they recited a spell. It wasn't long before she vanished into thin air! Captain N.H. soon left with his soldiers.

"I don't see why I had to let her go. She caused me so much suffering! Gabriel shook his head, still trying to figure out his ever-changing mission.

"You will in time," Walter replied as the two walked back in search of Captain N.H.

CHAPTER EIGHTEEN

Finding Captain N.H.

Walter and Gabriel walked down a path that would lead them back to the camp. "How's Abram?" Gabriel asked.

"He's fine. He's keeping an eye on things, too." Walter replied.

"Walter, you said you had faith in me! Why did you show up?" Gabriel asked.

"My boy, I have faith, I promise. I have faith in you, in others, The Land of Fenton! But, as your caretaker, it is my job to ensure your safety."

The two arrived at the campsite late that afternoon. The soldiers from both sides had all retreated for the day. Gabriel was greeted with a message from one of the soldiers.

"They have surrendered for the day but Captain N.H. says they will be back," the soldier told him while reading the message on parchment paper.

Gabriel nodded, and explored the surroundings as he tried to decide their next move. "Thank you," he told the soldier and continued through the campsite toward his tent with Walter.

Walter turned to Gabriel, "Have you decided how you're going to take back the crown?"

Gabriel shook his head, "I'm afraid I don't know. Fern says I have a heart, I just don't know how to use it."

"Go with your instincts and use the skills we have taught you," Walter reminded him.

Gabriel sighed heavily, "You're right, Walter. I promise I won't let you down."

The young boy went inside his tent. He stayed dressed but placed his sword and armor nearby. Gabriel rested his head on a pillow, and sleep finally came. He would be thankful for the sleep later.

By the next morning, Gabriel heard the sounds of the horses returning to the campsite once again. Gabriel grabbed his sword and shield. "Men, women, get ready!"

Immediately, on Gabriel's command, he watched as once again, his soldiers emerged from their tents, ready to fight. Dust continued to fill the area, making it almost impossible for anyone to see.

"Show yourself!" Gabriel hollered as he coughed from the dust.

"Tired of waiting?" came the reply.

Gabriel turned around to find his uncle on his white steed. He then looked at his uncle and said, "No! I'm tired of *you* hiding," Gabriel huffed.

Gabriel watched as Captain N.H. hopped off his horse and drew his sword from its sheath. "So, you want to fight with me, huh?"

After a few moments, Gabriel nodded. He kept his sword behind him for now. "Yes, I do." He replied calmly. "But first, I want you to tell me what happened to my parents!"

Captain N.H. stared at Gabriel for a long time. "Your parents?"

Gabriel looked at Captain N.H. He felt the anger building in his eyes. "Yes! Where are they? Did you kill them?"

A long, wicked laugh followed before Captain N.H. spoke again. "I don't owe you any explanation. However, if you really want to know, I'll tell you..."

CHAPTER NINETEEN

The Truth

It was late into the night when Matthew heard the noises of the Dagger-Baggers outside the Royal Castle. His wife, Eden stirred in their bed and yawned softly, "What is it, Matthew?" Eden wiped her eyes while her husband looked outside the window.

"Get dressed!" Matthew commanded his wife. "Get Gabriel to Abram, now! They've come for him, Eden."

Eden reached into her son's crib and pulled him out. He was fast asleep, even with the loud noises outside. "Come on, Gabriel. You're okay, my love."

As Matthew dressed, he quickly kissed the forehead of his son. "We'll be back soon, little guy."

Not long after dressing and taking their newborn son to Abram, Matthew, and Eden found themselves overtaken by the evil pirates. They were completely surrounded from every corridor of the Royal Castle. King Shamus was visiting a family member and therefore unable to help. Abram hid in a locked room with Gabriel in his arms. He softly wept as he held the young prince.

Eden gripped her husband's hand and whispered to him as they were dragged outside, "Where are they taking us?"

Matthew looked back and then looked ahead at the pirates leading them out of the Royal Castle and far, far into the forest, "I have no idea, my love."

The torches held by the pirates were the only light shining the way in the night. There was no moon and the clouds were covering any visibility of the stars that night. Up ahead, the torches showed a large, old carriage-trailer with bars on all sides.

"Get inside," griped one of the larger Dagger-Baggers to Eden and Matthew.

Turning to their right and then to their left, Matthew and Eden saw nowhere to run, so they stepped inside the abandoned carriage-trailer.

The Dagger-Baggers took Gabriel's parents to the outskirts of The Land of Fenton and tortured them for three months, demanding the two teach them the ways of their magic. The Dagger-Baggers wanted to use their powers for evil things.

"Just make it easy for yourselves!" A Dagger-Bagger said as he kicked Matthew. Eden cried as she watched her husband suffer.

With each new day, Matthew and Eden pleaded to be given their freedom, and each new day they were told the same thing, "If you tell us how to reverse the spell for animals to speak, you can go free!"

"I'm not teaching you anything," Eden told them every time she was brought an animal. The couple remained determined to keep the animals and The Land of Fenton safe from harm.

Matthew continued to hold out hope that someone somewhere would find them and save them. And he was right because someone was on the way.

The handsome man stood in front of the mirror as he looked at himself and pulled on his armor. His blond hair was long and curly, just barely covering his strong, hazel eyes. He knew his mission may be doomed to failure, but he had to at least try to save The Land of Fenton's Prince and Princess. He still felt incredibly guilty for not being at the Royal Castle when Matthew and Eden were captured.

Many others tried to save the two over the last few months. Unfortunately, all who tired failed, however. The man knew he was the last hope available at restoring peace to The Land of Fenton.

After fully dressing in his armor, a small knock came at his door. The tall man turned to it. "Yes, please enter," the man said.

A short man with a multi-colored robe entered. He was holding a baby. "I'm sorry to bother you, King Shamus, but I was hoping I might could talk you out of this one last time. After all, so many have failed to retrieve your son and daughter-in-law."

King Shamus smiled gently and walked toward his trusted advisor, "Thank you, Abram. We have been together for many years now. I'm capable of facing any trouble out there. Besides, what about the boy?" He pointed to the baby Abram held in his arm.

"But, sir," Abram protested. His words fell on deaf ears, unfortunately.

"Abram, please. I've made up my mind." King Shamus walked toward a window and looked out at the beautiful Kingdom. "You know, Abram, I've been giving this a lot of thought. It's time now that I pass on your role as my advisor to someone else."

Abram shook his head as he looked up at the tall King, "But, sir, I don't understand. Are you firing me?"

King Shamus walked toward Abram. He laughed and then lifted the baby out of the hands of Abram. He kissed his grandson on the forehead, "Hi, Gabriel!" King Shamus looked at his advisor for a long moment. He realized just how much he meant to him. He was his friend, too. "Absolutely not. I'm *freeing* you. I'm making you his godfather. Walter will remain his caretaker."

Abram was visibly moved, and a small tear left his eye. "Godfather? You're speaking like you won't be returning, sir!"

King Shamus handed Gabriel back to Abram. "I can't promise anything. I want to ensure Gabriel's safety. So, Abram, do we have an agreement?"

Abram looked as if he were going to pass out but nodded, "Yes, sir, of course. Thank you, King Shamus. It is an honor."

The King sighed heavily and there was silence for a long time. "There's one more thing. If something, anything at all should happen to me, you must take Gabriel to Harmony."

Abram looked at The King with a terrified face. "King Shamus, no! Sir, that's where individuals who abuse magic go. The Dagger-Baggers will find him. I can't take him there. His hair is as blond as yours and Matthew's. He may never come back!"

King Shamus remained quiet as he began to walk out of his room and the two walked down a long corridor of the beautiful castle. Finally, the two stopped in front of an empty frame. The King waved his hand over it after reciting a spell. Abram watched as a beautiful painting suddenly sprang to life. The painting, contained familiar sights from around The Land of Fenton. "Look at that handsome fella," King Shamus teased, looking at his own portrait in the painting.

"The painting may change as things change in The Land of Fenton. But, when, and if necessary, this oil canvas painting must go with Gabriel. Understood?" The King asked.

"No. Not understood, sir. Abram replied.

"The oil canvas painting will be Gabriel's portal into our World," The King explained. He then pulled out a large envelope and handed it to Abram. "This explains everything. You are to leave Gabriel with my daughter-in-law's sister. She was banished years ago. In my heart, I believe in second chances, just like our Creator. So, I believe she has learned the error of her ways after her own father died."

The two looked back at the painting, "You will be responsible for Gabriel. You will find a similar oil canvas painting in your cottage. Please have Walter accompany you on the journey to Harmony."

Abram nodded as The King continued to go over the plans.

"There's one more thing," King Shamus explained as he spoke to Abram.

Abram listened but sighed as he felt like he was hearing the last wishes of the powerful ruler. "I really hope it doesn't come to this and you come back with our Prince and Princess."

"I do, too, Abram," The King said in agreement. "I do, too."

CHAPTER TWENTY

The Risky Escape

The King traveled for three days and three nights searching for his son and daughter-in-law. He knew he was close to finding them, however, because he found Dagger-Bagger and horse tracks. It was widely known only Dagger-Baggers used horses for travel. Most of those in The Land of Fenton believed animals were equal to humans and therefore were never allowed to be used for such things.

King Shamus followed the tracks until he couldn't see them anymore when he found a large, damp cave. "Eureka," The King said as he approached it, quietly.

He quickly drew his sword from its sheath and walked into the cave. Several torches lined the interior cave. He had no idea what he may find as he walked inside. He refused to believe he would find the bodies of his son or daughter-in-law, however. He held out hope the two were still alive. His faith never yielded. As he neared the middle of the cave, he spotted a horrible sight. He put his sword away.

"Oh, my goodness!" he said in horror as he saw his son and daughter-in-law shackled together, severely beaten, but very much alive. He couldn't believe his eyes.

Matthew was the first to look up at his father. "Father, you're here," Matthew croaked out.

Eden looked up and saw her father-in-law. "Shamus!" King Shamus ran to Matthew and hugged his son the best he could and cried. "I couldn't leave you two behind. I'm so sorry I didn't come sooner!"

Matthew shook his head as he felt his father hold him through the hug.

"We don't have much time!" King Shamus said as he looked at his son and daughter-in-law. "I have a plan. Just trust me, okay?"

Matthew and Eden nodded, and King Shamus whispered the plan, quickly, quietly, and coherently. Suddenly, Eden looked behind her father-in-law, and screamed.

King Shamus turned toward her, "What is it, Eden?" She pointed to the source.

The tall, handsome king turned and saw a giant Dagger-Bagger towering high above him. The Dagger-Bagger held a dagger in his right hand. He looked like he was salivating.

"I will cut off your head with this dagger, and then I will bag it up," he laughed.

For a moment there was silence. Then, Matthew began to laugh, too. "Oh, that's funny! So, that's how you guys got your name?" He snorted, "It's cute, I'll give you that!"

Eden gently kicked her husband, "Not the time, Mattie!"

King Shamus drew his sword from his back and waved it toward the towering giant. "Not so fast, you pirate! We have love in our hearts. We aren't scared of you!"

From behind the giant, came a voice, "We only need one thing from you, Shamus, or rather, from you, Eden. Maybe she doesn't have to die."

"Who is that? Show yourself!" King Shamus demanded.

The giant stepped aside but continued to clutch his dagger and kept it pointed at The King. The torches lining the cave walls helped reveal a short man with a round belly.

"Prince N.H. at your service," the man said. He made a bowing motion, mocking The King.

"N.H., I should have known you were behind all of this," King Shamus said with his eyes fixed on the short man. "What do you want from us?"

Prince N.H. laughed and stepped closer to The King. "It's quite simple really. I want to know how your daughter-in-law teaches animals to speak. How do you do it, Eden? Teach us how to reverse it, and I will let you both go."

"My son, when did you become so evil?" The King replied, dodging the question. "You don't have to do this. Please, stop. You are loved, despite your wicked ways."

For a moment, it appeared N.H. was touched by his father's words. "Really, Daddy? That's all I ever…" he then began to laugh and jumped wildly until he grabbed the dagger out of the giant's hand. "Oh, boy! That was fun. Pretending to actually care about you. Now, answer my question! How do I reverse the spell?"

King Shamus looked at his son and daughter-in-law shackled together, defenseless. In his heart, he knew could give the spell to N.H., and the Dagger-Baggers would probably let them go, too. But, King Shamus also knew, this was Eden's spell to give. It was risky but King Shamus decided to stick to the original plan. "Alright, my son, we'll do it," King Shamus said to N.H.

"Shamus, no! Don't do it!" Eden hollered. "The animals will lose their abilities to speak. "We've worked so hard to help the animals! It can't be reversed, sir."

The King held up his hand to silence her.

N.H. laughed, "Good! I'm so glad we have reached an agreement." He stared Eden down and walked over to her and smiled. "The spell, please."

Eden shook her head. "Please! There has to be another way!"

"Just give it to him," The King begged.

Eden sighed and slowly began to recite the spell. N.H. rubbed his hands together with glee.

Suddenly a bright light appeared inside the cave and knocked N.H. down onto his feet. He slowly picked himself up from the cave floor, "What the...?" He looked over to see no sight of King Shamus. All that remained was a shield and sword. He walked over and hesitated for a moment before he lifted it and found a large, green frog wearing a crown. He was greeted with a loud croak.

"Hello, my son," the frog uttered.

N.H. backed up in fear of the frog. "What is going on here?" The frog hopped away and into the lap of Matthew.

"You see, my son, I knew you'd try to kill me as soon as you learned the spell to reverse animals learning to speak," The King beamed.

Captain N.H. shook his head, "But that doesn't explain why you're a frog now."

"If you'd let me finish, impatient one," The King said before continuing. "And, by turning into a frog, you cannot harm me for at least twelve years," The King laughed through a croak. "Great acting work, Eden," he smiled.

The King then lifted his new hands into the air. He recited a few words and the shackles suddenly loosened and broke away from the Prince and Princess. Eden and Matthew then took off running with King Shamus in tow.

When the three were far enough away from the Dagger-Baggers, Matthew put his father down on the ground.

"I can't believe we made it," Matthew said, nearly out of breath.

Eden smiled and looked down at her father-in-law but suddenly realized something painful, "Oh, no."

"What's wrong?" King Shamus said looking up at her from the ground below.

"I just realized that the human to animal spell is permanent even after the twelve years of invincibility ends."

King Shamus stared at his daughter-in-law for a long time before speaking to her. "It's alright, Eden. The fact you two are alive is more important to me than anything in this World. The secret to reversing the animals being able to speak remains hidden for now.

Eden bent down and picked up The Frog King and kissed him on the forehead. King Shamus blushed.

"I love you so much," Eden said with a big grin.

CHAPTER TWENTY-ONE

Having Faith

After Gabriel heard the events surrounding his parents capture and their escape, he shook his head, still having many questions. Only one seemed to matter at the moment, however.

"There's still one question that remains. What happened to my parents? Are they still alive?"

Captain N.H. stared back at Gabriel for a moment. "I never heard what happened to them, it was as if they vanished all together after that day."

Gabriel didn't know whether to believe him or not. Of course, in that moment, he had no reason to doubt him either.

Captain N.H. cleared his throat. "Look, kid, I get you're still grieving over Mommy and Daddy," he said sarcastically, "But I have a battle to win. I'd like to get a game of golf in later, if I can!"

Gabriel looked up at him. "Oh. Right." At that moment, the young boy suddenly didn't feel as determined to win. He felt like an orphan after holding out hope for so long that his parents may be alive. Suddenly, he felt a cool breeze hit him in the face.

"What's that?" he asked softly. He looked to his right and saw Fern in the ocean, smiling at him. "You're here!" Gabriel exclaimed as he looked over at her.

"Of course," she giggled. "And you need to fight with that heart of yours!"

Gabriel protested, "But, Fern, he just told me the news I have been dreading for so long. My parents are..." but Gabriel couldn't finish.

Fern looked at him and tilted her head, "You don't know that," she snapped. "Stop letting him beat you before the battle is even over!"

Gabriel nodded and sighed heavily, "Thanks, Fern." He turned back to Captain N.H. and drew his sword from its sheath. "You want a battle, I'll give you a battle."

Captain N.H. chuckled, wickedly. "You still think you can beat me, huh?"

Gabriel shook his head, "I have faith. I have the power of good and you are forgetting about my soldiers. We have love in our hearts!" His sword touched his uncle's. "So, the question is, how much faith do you have?"

Captain N.H. laughed, "I don't need faith, Gabriel. I have my own power, and soon I'll have yours, too!"

The two men's swords continued to clack back and forth. Captain N.H. was the same height as Gabriel and being overweight, he paled in speed, but his magic helped him move around. The two moved their swords around with loud whacks and clacks.

Other soldiers and pirates joined in on the fight. There was no turning back now. Gabriel knew his soldiers had to win. He was determined to win this fight for his parents and grandfather. He wanted to make this man pay for what he had done to their family.

Suddenly, the sword from Captain N.H. came driving toward Gabriel, but he quickly blocked the attack from his uncle with his shield.

Captain N.H. laughed again. "What are you trying to prove, Gabriel?" he asked with a smile that reminded him of his Uncle Mort whenever he made a seedy business deal.

"That good can and will win over evil! I won't dishonor my grandfather," Gabriel said, without a hint of fear in his voice.

Gabriel then drove his sword as close as he could to his uncle. At the same moment, his uncle drove his sword as close as he could to his nephew. Their swords flew out of their hands. The two then exchanged blows on the ground below without their swords, only their fists. Soldiers all around suddenly stopped fighting and hollered and cheered.

It was over quickly enough, however, and both were back on their feet, grabbing their swords.

"No, we fight like men!" Gabriel said as he dusted himself off. "We finish this the real way!"

Captain N.H. laughed at his nephew, "You? A man? Ha!" He laughed so hard he didn't see his nephew approaching him. "Uh oh…"

Gabriel drove back with his own sword and drove it into the man's rib, Captain N.H. fell to the ground.

Gabriel pulled the sword back, looked at Captain N.H., and stared him in the eyes. Captain N.H. began gasping for breath. "You got me, Gabriel," Captain N.H. said.

"Does that mean you give up?" Gabriel uttered as he cleaned his sword in the ground. He then placed his sword back into its sheath.

He watched Captain N.H. cough and scuttle across the ground. For a moment he felt sorry for his uncle. He didn't know if he should help him or not. He decided to at least try. He reached for the man's hand.

Before he could help his uncle, he watched as the man suddenly vanished from sight. Gabriel spun around multiple times, "Where'd he go now!?"

CHAPTER TWENTY-TWO

Where He Went

The three sat at a long table inside Walter and Abram's cottage. "You see, Gabriel, sometimes when someone gets wounded, they can use a spell to help themselves," Walter explained to Gabriel. "It's a cheap tactic, but what do you expect from your uncle?" Walter popped a piece of a dinner roll into his mouth as he, Abram and Gabriel ate dinner that evening.

Gabriel shook his head. "But I was *this* close to defeating him. He's still king, too! I failed! What will I to do now?"

Abram touched his godson's shoulder "You didn't fail. I'm sure we can get him next time! Besides, don't forget the

Dagger-Baggers fled in fear over your fight with N.H., too! Your troops even made sure they flooded the pirate's ships. Now, their ships will have to limp back to Harmony before they founder." Abram explained gently.

"I guess that's a good thing. Where do we find my uncle now?" Gabriel asked.

Walter and Abram were silent for a moment, exchanging a look. Walter then sighed, scooped out more peas, and put them on Gabriel's plate. "Gabriel, my boy, we will find a way to defeat him. He's a difficult being. Nobody said this would be easy."

Abram gestured toward the wall behind him after a long, uncomfortable silence. Gabriel looked to see there was a duplicate oil canvas painting, "How'd you get that?" Gabriel asked.

Abram shook his head, "Listen, Gabriel. As much as we love having you here, our advice is to make your way back to Harmony."

Gabriel's jaw dropped, "You're making me go back?"

Walter shook his head, "No, Gabriel! But, see, there's a reason you need to go back. You will find out more when you get there."

Gabriel protested a little longer, "I don't understand. I thought my fight was here. What good could come from me going back to Harmony? I want to stay here and fight Captain N.H. and get my grandfather's throne back."

Walter explained a little more, "No. Your training was here. Your fight, well, it's only just begun."

The young boy stood from the table, visibly upset, "This is unfair!" His hand hit the table with more force than he intended.

Abram stood up, "Now, hold on, Gabriel. Don't get upset!"

"No! I am upset. It's as if you two don't believe in me, and now you're kicking me out!" Gabriel was fuming at the words spoken to him.

"We're not kicking you out, Gabriel. You just have to trust us on this," Walter explained.

Gabriel started to tear up, "How can I trust you, when you won't even explain to me what's going on?"

Abram stepped forward and started to wave his hand over his godson. Gabriel grabbed hold of Abram by his fist.

"No. Not this time," Gabriel said, still pretty angry.

Abram nodded, "We will be with you there eventually, just as we were there in the very beginning. However, Gabriel, you must go ahead of us."

Gabriel sighed as he sat back down, submitting to the two men's demands, "When am I going? And what about my aunt? Won't she try to hurt me? What about my uncle?"

Walter snickered, "You're forgetting that a banished being is weaker in Harmony than they are back here."

Abram jumped in, "And you're leaving as soon as you finish your dinner. Eat, eat, please."

Gabriel grumbled but continued to eat, figuring that all of his questions would be answered in time. In his heart, he wished the dinner would never end and he could stay in The Land of Fenton for forever.

After dinner, the three walked to the familiar oil canvas painting. Gabriel stared for a long time.

"Well…" Abram said looking at Gabriel.

"Well…" Walter said.

The two men looked at one another and then at Gabriel. It was obvious they were hoping they could be talked out of Gabriel leaving, even if his going was part of the greater plan to take down Captain N.H. and his pirates once and for all.

"I don't understand how this will all be worked out. Won't they wonder where I've been the last nine months?" Gabriel asked, still confused.

"You are giving them too much credit. Besides, your aunt was here, too," Abram pointed out.

"That's true," Gabriel replied.

Gabriel hugged Abram tightly. "I know this isn't for forever, but I'm going to miss you so much. Promise me will see each other as soon as possible."

Abram nodded as they hugged, "You can count on it."

As they released their hug, they both wiped tears away from the other, one last time.

Walter was next. Gabriel hugged his caretaker tightly. Walter reached into his cloak and handed him the familiar key. "Remember, you have the key to your Aunt Marge getting back here, as I said." He smiled through the hug. As they pulled away he added, "Don't let her take this key away from you."

Gabriel nodded and put the key into his pocket. He finally understood why the caretaker asked him to let her go back to Harmony. It was where she belonged. "I won't. I promise."

Gabriel turned back toward the oil canvas painting and then looked back at Walter and Abram. "These really were some great adventures. I'm sure there will be more in the future. I learned a lot about myself. I learned that I'm loved, and I'm capable of loving, too," Gabriel said to the two men.

"Of course, there will be more adventures," Walter said. "Life, my boy, is an adventure!"

Gabriel approached the painting but was interrupted by Abram.

"Wait! There's one more thing!" Abram produced a small envelope. "Take this with you!"

The young boy studied the envelope, "What is this?"

Abram shook his head, "Don't open it now. It's for later."

With a heavy sigh, Gabriel nodded, and then placed a hand into the painting, feeling the familiar coolness on the other side. As he studied the painting, he suddenly had one more thought. "Fern..." Gabriel quietly uttered.

He turned back, and Abram nodding his head, knowingly said, "I'll tell her."

"She was the one who assured me about the love in my heart. She told me that being afraid would get me nowhere," Gabriel confessed.

"Where do you think she gets her smarts?" Abram snorted.

Gabriel laughed, "Well, that's definitely true. Tell her I will come back again soon enough."

Abram nodded but reassured his godson, "She knows, Gabriel."

Gabriel turned back to the oil canvas painting. He hesitated.

"Go on, Gabriel," Walter encouraged him.

"Goodbye, Abram. Goodbye, Walter," Gabriel said one last time.

The two men said their goodbyes and waved. Gabriel stepped through the painting and was gone, leaving Abram and Walter behind.

Abram turned to Walter after a long beat of silence between the two. "Walter, should we have explained more to the boy? Should we have explained more about why his training was here in The Land of Fenton? Don't you think we should have told him why his real mission is back in Harmony?"

Walter shook his head no.

Abram stared at the painting and then looked back at his friend. "Walter, there's something you should know."

Walter looked at Abram, "What is it?"

Abram hesitated for a moment and bit his bottom lip. "I know what happened to Gabriel's parents."

The men walked away from the painting and an overdue discussion was exchanged between two friends.

CHAPTER TWENTY-THREE

Three Months Later

Gabriel was unsure when he'd ever get back to The Land of Fenton again, but he knew he had the only key to the room with the oil canvas painting if he ever decided to try again, should the moment arise. He just hoped that Walter and Abram's promise to find him in the future was true.

Gabriel realized that even though he may not have defeated his uncle, he learned a lot from his time in The Land of Fenton. He learned that while he grew up feeling different and neglected, he was destined for great things. His grandfather told him so. Besides his home in Harmony wasn't a forever home anyhow.

He reached into his pocket and pulled out the key. He held it tightly. In his other pocket he pulled out the envelope from Abram. "I guess there's no harm opening it now, right?" Gabriel asked himself. He tore it open, and inside, he found a photo from his first birthday party.

In the photo, Gabriel stood in the middle of Walter and Abram. That was his real family. The people outside the walls of his bedroom weren't his family. They didn't have love in their hearts like Abram, Walter, and Fern.

Abram and Walter taught him so much about love in the short time he knew them. He couldn't wait to be reunited once again.

He spent most of his time in his bedroom reading spells that Abram had taught him so he could stay on top of his training. He also spent time reading from the big book and all about the Creator. He had to keep his books hidden. He knew his aunt was unable to go to and from The Land of Fenton now, however, thanks to the ships foundering.

Yes, while Gabriel wasn't any closer to finding out more information about the fate of his parents, he felt when the time was right, he would return to The Land of Fenton to dig deeper and learn the truth. "I'll go back to find them, someday. As long as there are talking animals out there, I know they are still alive. They have to be," Gabriel smiled to himself. "But I'm coming back to find you, Mom and Dad. I promise."

One evening, Gabriel was in his bedroom, he heard his uncle outside his bedroom. Mort loudly banged on the door.

"Get out here, Gabriel! Now!" Mort shouted.

"What's wrong?" Gabriel asked as he opened the door.

Uncle Mort smiled for the first time in his nephew's presence, "The Mayor has an important message to make on television. So, get out here and come watch with us," Uncle Mort insisted.

Gabriel yawned and stumbled out into the living room. No one outside his aunt knew of his adventures, and he didn't intend to tell anyone about them either. Gabriel sat on the floor as the news conference began.

A familiar face to the residents of Harmony approached a podium. The man was short, with very little hair, and a round belly. The few hairs he had were greying. The man was a celebrity in Harmony. He was admired not just for his military service, his co-founding of Harmony, but also his leadership as Harmony's mayor. There was one young boy, however, who had never met him.

As the man approached the podium, it was easy to see for others that he wasn't quick with his steps. This man was Mayor Norm Hull. Although he walked with a smile, Gabriel noticed he also clutched his right rib. Gabriel thought that was a little odd. Mayor Hull reached the podium to speak. Before he even began his words, there was loud applause from those in attendance at his press conference.

"My fellow citizens of Harmony, thank you! I come to you on a momentous occasion. I am excited to inform you we are lifting the two-child policy on all households, effective immediately." Mayor Norm Hull began to smile again as the crowds applauded him enthusiastically. Bright flash bulbs blurred the television screen. Loud chants from those in attendance at the press conference began praising their leader for his landmark decision.

"Now, I know many of you are wondering why I have chosen to make this decision. Well, I have realized it was a foolish law. I have realized that I, your mayor, can be wrong about such things. The long and short is, I have learned all of this, thanks in large part to one person in particular."

Gabriel looked around the living room as the family watched the speech. He spotted Gretel and Gus and his Uncle Mort but saw no sign of his aunt. He cleared his throat, "Hey, Uncle Mort, where is Aunt Marge?"

Uncle Mort hushed him but quickly replied, "You didn't hear? She started a new job today."

Gabriel turned back to the television as Mayor Hull continued working the crowd with his speech. "This individual helped me out years ago when we were serving together in the military. Back then I was known as N.H. Back then I even had an awful hair piece." He touched his balding head.

"Service will do mighty cruel things to a man's hair," he laughed at his own, lame joke.

The crowd laughed at his comment, too.

"Oh, no!" Gabriel said, with a lump in his throat, realizing the truth.

"Hush, Gabriel," Gus said.

Mayor Hull continued, "I'd like to take this opportunity to once again thank this fine lady for helping me see the errors of my ways. Marge Canton, my humble servant, citizens of Harmony, will be Harmony's new deputy mayor!" Mayor Norm Hull said to thunderous applause. Gabriel saw the camera pan over to his aunt. She walked over, and the two exchanged a hug and a soft kiss on the cheek given by his aunt.

Aunt Marge walked to the podium and adjusted the microphone to her level, "Thank you, Mayor Norm Hull. Or as I remember you, Captain."

The crowed laughed again.

Gabriel stared at the television screen in horror as she spoke to the crowd and the residents watching at home. Marge continued speaking. "I'm so glad you overturned this law, Mr. Mayor, because now it allows us to finally open our minds, our hearts, and, yes, even our homes. Now, under this new law reversal, we don't have to worry about hiding secrets. Not that we have any."

Gabriel's uncle and cousins began to laugh at his aunt's joke along with all those in attendance at the press conference. He didn't laugh, however. He watched, terrified.

As Gabriel watched Aunt Marge speak, he thought for a moment that he saw his aunt wink at the camera, but he couldn't be sure...

PART TWO

"We live in a world in which we need to share responsibility. It's easy to say, 'It's not my child, not my community, not my world, not my problem.' Then, there are those who see the need and respond. I consider those people my heroes."

- FRED ROGERS

CHAPTER TWENTY-FOUR

His Arrival

Marge waited inside Mayor Norm Hull's office. She eagerly looked around the room. "Any minute now, he'll be back." Marge snickered to herself as she recalled her memories from back in The Land of Fenton. She paced around the room, back and forth, back and forth. Her eagerness grew stronger and stronger with each step around the office. What a thrill the memories were of tormenting Gabriel, and the two were just getting started!

The groundwork had been set. First, Marge made herself look vulnerable for Gabriel. She quivered, admitted defeat, and allowed Mayor Hull time to send her back to Harmony by reciting a spell. Then, Mayor Hull, himself, would allow Gabriel to get the upper hand long enough so he'd have time to cast a spell to disappear, too. All of these false illusions of winning would soon be revealed. Marge knew this would lure Gabriel back to Harmony and set the trap. They knew once back in Harmony, they could ensure Gabriel would play by their own rules, not his own.

Indeed, the idea for the plan was made years ago when Marge decided to tell Mayor Hull about her nephew. She knew with his wicked past and her strong powers, together, they could take down the family that made both their lives miserable for a long, long time. Marge and Mayor Hull believed Gabriel would be less likely to perform his magic in Harmony and would be much weaker as a result. Back in Harmony, they could defeat him, once and for all.

As Marge walked around the office, Mayor Hull's desk phone rang. Being the gossip she was, Marge didn't hesitate from walking over to the desk to pick it up. "Hello?" Marge said in a phony sweet tone. She couldn't wait to hear from her supreme leader. She knew he would have plenty to say. Her phony voice was quickly broken, however, when an all too familiar voice spoke.

"Hello, hon. It's your husband." the voice uttered back into the headset. "I tried to reach you on your cell, but there was no answer. So, on a whim, I tried Mayor Hull."

Marge covered the phone to let out an annoyed grunt as she pushed back her brown hair, which was coarse and unkempt, unlike her nephew's beautiful, blond hair. She tried to think of a lie for ignoring his call only minutes before. She uncovered the mouth piece. "Mort, baby!" Marge gushed as she said his name. "How I have missed you!" Being out of sight of her husband, she quickly made a gag motion with her finger when she caught glimpse of herself in a mirror.

"Really now?" Mort replied. "You go all the way to The Land of Fenton and don't even try to contact me?"

Marge looked at her reflection, trying to come up with another plausible lie. She snickered when one came to her so quickly. "Now, now, sweet husband! You know you're still my favorite Dagger-Bagger." Marge knew just how to stroke her husband's ego. It was working beautifully, too.

Any knucklehead with half a brain would know everything Marge was saying was lies. Unfortunately, Mort was buying the whole charade. He wasn't very smart, after all.

Mort chuckled and kissed the mouthpiece of his phone. "I know. Gosh, I just wish I could've seen the look on that little kid's face. I wish you and Mayor Hull would have included me on the mission to take down Gabriel."

Marge smiled before speaking again. "Oh, Mort! You're in luck! The mission has just begun!"

"Wait! What do you mean?" Mort asked quickly, obviously more confused than ever. "I don't understand."

"You will in time. Just know that your efforts so far have been very, very helpful."

"Yeah, but…" Mort tried to cut in.

Marge spoke over her husband, "Well, I have to go! Kiss!" Marge replied and placed the phone back on its cradle.

Marge blew out a big sigh of relief. "I can't have him ruin the plan when I'm so close to winning," she uttered out loud as she began pacing around the room once again.

"No. You can't. But who said *you're* close to winning? I thought *we* were close to winning," pointed out the voice behind her.

"Mayor Hull!" Marge spun around to spot her leader sitting behind his desk, still in his battlefield gear. He appeared to be nursing a wound on or near his right rib.

"Yes, yes. It's me, my humble servant," Mayor Hull replied, as if he were a celebrity. He leaned against the back support of his chair, smirking.

Marge smiled as she rushed to him. She soon spotted the wound and confirmed it to be his right rib. "Oh, dear! Mayor Hull! You're hurt!" she exclaimed.

Mayor Hull shook his head, "Don't worry about it! I'm fine. Our plan is still very much intact. However, there is one important thing we need to do!"

Marge tilted her head. "Oh? What's that?"

The Mayor smiled and grabbed his phone from his desk. He snickered as he punched the button for Human Resources. "Make you my new Deputy Mayor."

Marge let out an evil laugh.

CHAPTER TWENTY-FIVE

Discussions Made

The two spent the next three months discussing their perfect plan in secret. A press conference was planned for later in the afternoon to announce the reversal of the two-child policy and also to introduce Marge as Mayor Hull's new deputy mayor.

"The reversal will allow our residents to be on the lookout for him! He can roam the streets and our residents, our Dagger-Baggers, can find him and bring him to us!" Mayor Hull said with a laugh.

"But we will also create a false sense of security for him. We will make him think he can leave the house at any time he wants. Then, boom!" Marge said with a loud voice. She pushed her right fist into her open left hand.

"I just wish I could see Gabriel's face," Mayor Hull said, and went over a few, last minute items. "But we'll be doing this press conference on television, so I'll miss it!"

"I wish I could see his face, too!" Marge laughed with an evil smile. "But I do plan to wink at the camera. Then, the pathetic soul will know we're watching him."

"Oh, that's a pretty subtle, yet perfect way to grab his attention," Mayor Hull said while rubbing his hands together with a nod.

"I'll need to tell Mort about this part of the plan," Marge explained, as she bit her bottom lip.

Mayor Hull agreed.

Mayor Hull laughed along with Marge. "So, let's go over the plan one last time to be sure it's understood, shall we? We have to make sure the plan goes perfectly so there's not a sneak attack."

Marge nodded in agreement.

After the press conference, Gabriel rose to his feet and turned to his cousins and uncle. The looks on their faces told him everything he needed to know. They were silent for a long time. Gabriel was afraid to speak so he only stood there, motionless.

"Don't be afraid," Gretel finally said with a small hint of a smile.

"Well, he can be afraid of me," Gus added. "Why do you think I chased you through the oil canvas painting, Pea Brain?"

Gabriel swallowed heavily in his throat. "So, you were part of the plan?" He croaked, unable to ask anything else.

His uncle stood up, in between his two children, and patted both of them on the back. "Careful! We don't want him to run away!" Mort said, with a smile, and a wink at Gabriel, making him think back to the press conference.

"Don't worry, Gabriel! We're not going to harm you. Remember, we can't perform magic after being banished from The Land of Fenton. Well, we're not supposed to, anyhow. Sometimes, if we're not careful, it just slips."

Gabriel tilted his head, putting it together, "You're Dagger-Baggers, aren't you? Wait! Is everyone in Harmony a Dagger-Bagger?"

"Well, technically, Mom and Dad are Dagger-Baggers. Gus and I are Dagger-Baggers in training," Gretel pointed out with a laugh.

"And we're training quietly. As Dad said, we aren't supposed to be learning magic!" Gretel smirked.

Gus jumped in, "But, yes, everyone here was once banished from The Land of Fenton, Pea Brain! Unless they were born here and never got to experience the 'wonderful' world of The Land of Fenton," he added sarcastically with an eye roll.

Gabriel just stared at his cousins and uncle, "So, if you're not going to harm me, what are you going to do?"

"It's quite simple, really," Mort began, "We are going to keep you here until Mayor Hull and your Aunt Marge are ready for you."

Gabriel's confidence returned, "You can't do that! Don't forget I have the key, and the oil canvas painting is my portal to The Land of Fenton! I can leave at any time!"

Gretel stepped in, "Oh, poor, pathetic Gabriel. You haven't heard, have you?"

Gus snickered, but didn't say anything.

"Heard what?" Gabriel asked, while tilting his head. Gus looked like he was ready to add to the conversation and raised a finger and his lips began to move. Suddenly, however, Gabriel didn't want to hear. The sounds of their laughter from before told Gabriel he didn't need to stick around to wonder what they were going to add to the thought.

In that instant, Gabriel rushed to his bedroom. He dug through his cot until he retrieved the key. "Oh, thank goodness," he sighed. He waited a minute before exiting his room. He reached into his pocket and pulled out the picture of Walter and Abram.

"I'll see you soon," he said to the two men. He stared at their faces as he held the photo in his hand. "I can't wait to see you," he added. He shoved the photo back into his back pocket and exited his room, walking down the long, narrow hallway.

He approached the third door. He kept the key in his pocket until he reached his target. He heard his cousins and uncle still laughing about his aunt's speech.

"You can laugh, but I have the key," Gabriel huffed. He pulled out the key, and just as before, the key turned itself, and the door swung open. The key popped out and fell on to the floor. Everything seemed normal. He could already smell Walter's breakfast. He couldn't wait to see Fern. His cheeks blushed just at the thought. Once he was sure no one was near him, Gabriel bent down and picked up the key from the floor below. He put it into his front pocket for safekeeping.

However, something was very different than the last time he visited the room. Gabriel stepped inside the room. He looked to his left, and to his right as he'd done once before. This time, he didn't find a sheet covering a magical oil canvas painting. That's because there wasn't an oil canvas painting at all. His worst fear was true: the oil canvas painting was gone!

CHAPTER TWENTY-SIX

A Flash

Gabriel frantically ran out of the room and through the long corridor. He finally made his way back into the living room. When he reached his uncle and cousins, he was out of breath. He wanted answers, and he wanted them quickly.

"Uncle Mort!" Gabriel hollered loudly after catching his breath, nearly knocking his uncle out of his chair.

His uncle looked at him, annoyed, and then glanced back at his television program and turned up the volume to ignore him.

His cousins were seated on the sofa with their eyes glued to the television. Gabriel realized he wasn't going to get through to them and left the room, angrier than when he arrived.

"Forget it!" Gabriel yelled and ran back to his bedroom, shut the door, and locked it. He kicked the door with his foot. He then took the now useless key to the room containing the oil canvas painting and threw it against the wall. The key made a loud noise as it bounced from the wall and fell on to the floor below. Gabriel fell against the frame of his cot and began to cry. "She must've had other copies made," Gabriel decided. He hollered and bit his lip, trembling, "It's not fair! It's not fair!"

Gabriel looked around the small room as he tried to figure out something or anything he could to get out of this horrible situation. It was then he realized how much he missed Walter and Abram. He reached into his back pocket and pulled out the photo of Abram and Walter from his first birthday party. He sniffled as he wiped a few tears from his eyes. The tears returned again as he looked at the photo.

"You two always knew what to do in a crisis! What should I do, Walter?" Gabriel asked the tall, older gentleman in the photo. He then looked at the shorter man with the multi-colored robe. "What should I do, Abram?" He began to cry a third time. When he did, a single tear dropped from his eye and on to Abram's portrait. "Oh, no!" Gabriel frantically used his sleeve to clean the photo.

At that moment, Gabriel's still-boarded-up bedroom and the entire foundation of the Canton home, began to shake violently. Was this an earthquake? Dagger-Baggers are responsible for all of the natural disasters, Gabriel remembered.

The young boy grabbed hold of his cot's post to support his weight. "Hold on!" Gabriel told himself. "What's happening?" He heard noises from outside his bedroom soon after the noises and the shaking began.

"Gabriel, knock it off! We know you are causing that sound! Gabriel! Gabriel! Gabriel!" Uncle Mort pounded on Gabriel's door and yelled from the other side. The banging from the outside the door grew louder and louder. The shaking of the house grew more and more violent along with it. He heard the doorknob turn over and over again, but the door never opened.

Suddenly, Gabriel looked toward the right-hand wall and saw a silhouette of two figures, and a blinding flash appear. He studied and approached it slowly. He wasn't able to get too close before he was knocked back and on to his cot. The light grew brighter as he lay on his bed, still studying the light.

"What is that thing?" Gabriel said, his eyes still stunned by its illumination.

The noises from outside the door continued to grow louder and louder as the blinding flash slowly began to dim, and Gabriel began to smile.

CHAPTER TWENTY-SEVEN

Welcome Guests

Gabriel slid off his cot and stared at the two figures standing before him. "Walter! Abram!" Gabriel shouted with glee as he rushed to hug them.

Abram chuckled, hugging Gabriel tightly and removed the remaining tears away from his godson's eyes by simply running a hand over his face.

Walter stood to the side and smiled as he looked on at the scene.

Gabriel released his hug from Abram and suddenly tilted his head. "Wait a minute! How did you get here? The oil canvas painting is missing!"

Abram chuckled once again. "You really don't understand just how powerful your tears are, do you, my boy?"

Gabriel shook his head. "I guess I don't. What do you mean?"

Walter looked at Abram, as if asking for permission to explain what happened. Abram nodded for him to tell.

"Well, when your tears fell on the photo it summoned us here. Your tears and Abram's are connected on such a strong level that any time your heart feels so strongly for the other, not even the absence of the oil canvas painting can separate you two," Walter explained.

Gabriel stared in shock as Walter explained the situation to him. Before he could reply, Abram started speaking.

"Believe me, Gabriel, I wasn't sure about it either! One minute, I was relaxing in my favorite chair, looking over my spell book, and then I felt our cottage shake. Next thing I know, Walter and I are standing here with you."

Gabriel smiled wildly. "I can't believe it! You mean to tell me that you came here from The Land of Fenton just because of my tears? That's incredible!"

The two men nodded and shared a group hug with Gabriel. Walter adjusted his robe. "Alright, alright! Time to get down to business! We understand the oil canvas painting is gone, but I take it that's not the only issue. What else is going on?"

Gabriel sighed heavily. "Well, shortly after I got back, I found out Captain N.H. is actually Mayor Norm Hull."

"Well, Abram and I already knew that." Walter replied, with a clearing of his throat.

"You did? Why didn't you tell me?" Gabriel asked, looking over at Abram who looked ashamed at the floor below.

Abram slowly looked up, "Well, we thought it was best you find out on your own. That was one of the reasons we insisted you go back. Remember?"

Gabriel nodded, "Well, anyway, Mayor Hull lifted the two-child policy, so I assume I'm free to move about the house or go out in public, but it won't be so easy seeing as how everyone in Harmony is a Dagger-Bagger."

"Again, we already knew that. Get to the point, my boy." Walter asked, begging Gabriel to continue.

Gabriel sighed, "Okay, well, I then found out my Uncle Mort and cousins are keeping me here until my Aunt Marge and Mayor Hull are ready for me."

Abram scratched his chin. "Well, you know they are forbidden from doing magic here in Harmony. Of course, the rule doesn't stop them, usually, so it is a big deal, I suppose. The trick is making sure they don't get back to The Land of Fenton without you knowing. That must be why you're worried, huh?"

Walter rolled his eyes, "Yes, Abram, I think that's what the boy is worried about!" Walter groaned as he bopped the shorter man on the head.

"Ouch!" Abram rubbed the back of his head.

Gabriel nodded slowly, "Yes, that is why I'm worried. I'm sure the oil canvas painting is somewhere. I don't think they just threw it away or destroyed it." He sighed before continuing, "We have to find a way to take down Aunt Marge and lure Mayor Hull back to The Land of Fenton on our own terms. Obviously, lifting the two-child policy is a trap, so we have to be careful."

Walter looked at the boy, a bit confused by one of Gabriel's demands, "Why do you want to bring Norm Hull back to The Land of Fenton?"

"Because I believe he knows where my parents are," Gabriel began. "I think he knows a lot more than he told me the first time back in The Land of Fenton on the battlefield."

Abram looked back at Walter. "Well, actually…" Abram began, but was quickly cut off by Walter.

"We think that's a great idea!" Walter shot an eye at Abram to hush.

Gabriel nodded, "Thanks."

Walter sighed as he looked around the small room without windows, "Well, your father is next in line for the throne. But if we can't find him, your uncle will remain the tyrannical King of The Land of Fenton. We can't keep him as Mayor of Harmony and King of The Land of Fenton, too! We have to ensure your uncle doesn't get back to The Land of Fenton and take the throne permanently!"

Abram and Gabriel nodded in agreement.

Marge and Mayor Hull sat in a conference room inside Harmony's Municipal Building, further discussing their plans to take down Gabriel once and for all. No member of Harmony's council ever dared to question why regular government business was put on hold indefinitely. After all, Mayor Hull knew what was best for Harmony. The citizens respected that.

"So, you and Mort took care of the oil canvas painting, I assume?" Marge asked as she closed her daily planner, clicking her pen nervously.

Mayor Hull scratched his balding head and smiled. "Oh, of course. The oil canvas painting is in very, very safe hands."

Marge slowly nodded, "Good. We have to keep it in our possession since the spell to disappear between Harmony and The Land of Fenton only works one time per person," she reminded her leader.

Mayor Hull understood, "I'm well aware. It's safe. Do not worry."

"Are you going to tell me where it is?" Marge inquired.

Mayor Hull stood up from his seat, chuckled, and winked at Marge. "Follow me, Madam Deputy Mayor. Follow me."

The two walked out of the conference room and down the long hallway. Phones were ringing loudly, and voices were heard in room after room that was passed. They entered Mayor Hull's large office after the long walk.

"I don't understand. I don't see anything," Marge said with a puzzled look on her face. She watched Mayor Hull sit down behind his desk.

"Look closer," Mayor Hull said as he pushed a button from under his desk without Marge knowing.

Marge stood in awe as a painting of Mayor Hull suddenly lifted into the ceiling above and another one appeared in its place. Marge smiled when she saw the familiar oil canvas painting.

"Wow! That's pretty cool!" Marge gasped.

Mayor Hull chuckled again as he pushed the button. This caused the oil canvas painting to be replaced with his official Mayoral painting once again! Mayor Hull showed the button to Marge. "The best part is if this button is pushed by anyone other than yours truly, it will trigger a silent alarm. The silent alarm will alert a team of Dagger-Baggers here immediately!"

"Genius!" Marge smiled. "I have to be honest, I really want to push the button, though!"

Norm Hull grinned, "And when the moment is right, I will return to The Land of Fenton and take the throne permanently. But not until I deal with Gabriel here in Harmony!"

Marge just laughed, "That's perfect!"

Mayor Hull shook his head, "And to think my brother Matthew was called the smart son!"

CHAPTER TWENTY-EIGHT

Young Again

Walter shook his head as he stood with his back against a wall. He folded his arms across his chest and barked, "No! No! Absolutely not!"

"Well, I don't see how you expect to leave this room then," Abram replied. "Come on, we have to do it!"

Gabriel looked at his two friends and laughed softly, "Walter, I think he's right."

The two older men bickered back and forth over and over for a few more minutes. Walter didn't want to use any magic in Harmony for fear of getting caught doing it. Abram knew it had to be used, especially in their current situation.

"Come on, you used it that one time!" Abram begged.

Walter suddenly turned redder than a crisp, red apple. "You swore you'd never tell that story ever again!"

"And I won't as long as you agree to go along with my plan," Abram snapped back.

Walter groaned, realizing he finally lost an argument to his much shorter friend. "Fine! But only now, and in the future when absolutely necessary."

"Agreed," Abram said excitedly, beginning to raise his hands, about to begin the spell. He was beaming as he jumped in the air.

"I'm serious, Abram," Walter said, raising his eyebrow. "Absolutely necessary!"

Abram sighed heavily, "Fine, Walter! You win! Only when 'absolutely necessary!'"

Walter cleared his throat, "Thank you."

The two men put their hands together and closed their eyes and began to recite a spell that was unfamiliar to

Gabriel. He watched in amazement as a cloud of smoke filled the small room. Gabriel began to wave his hand over his face and coughed softly.

"Did it work?" Walter asked. His voice was very familiar, yet his physique was not.

Gabriel stared at the two men who were no longer two men at all. They were now two much younger versions of themselves.

"Whoa!" Gabriel replied as he looked at the two of them.

The plan was to sneak out of the bedroom and out of the house without Gabriel's uncle and cousins noticing. If he walked out with Walter and Abram in their true forms, he wouldn't be allowed out of the house. He knew it was possible his aunt or his uncle may recognize Abram and Walter from The Land of Fenton. Thanks to Norm Hull lifting the two-child policy, he was now allowed to leave the house freely. Well, that is, if he could sneak past his uncle.

Gabriel began to pack up a few things into a small backpack as Walter and Abram continued to bicker with one another.

"I hope this will work," Walter said as he pushed his new wire-rimmed glasses on his nose. His new body was still thin and tall, but he had curly-red hair. It was a bit messy, just like his old hair. His skin tone was pale and covered in freckles. His clothes were casual in fashion: khaki-colored shorts and a collared shirt.

"It will. It will. You need to trust me, Walter," Abram groaned. His personality was unchanged. He was dressed in blue jeans and a red V-neck t-shirt. Abram's brown eyes were already beautiful, but, in his younger state, looked almost chocolate in color.

Finally, Gabriel finished packing his bag, and the three made their way out of the small, dark bedroom. His uncle and cousins were still watching television as the three made their way closer and closer to the front door. As they reached the door, Gabriel began to think he wouldn't have to worry about being discovered.

"Going somewhere?" Uncle Mort asked. He could see Gabriel's reflection through the television screen but not the other two.

"Out. But I will be back soon." Gabriel replied. He would be back. So, it wasn't a lie, Gabriel rationalized.

Uncle Mort kept his eyes on the television, never turning to see the three of them.

"Okay! Don't give me a reason to have to come get you!" Uncle Mort finally said as he turned up the volume on the television.

Gabriel carefully opened the door and walked out. Walter closed it behind him once the three of them were outside.

Suddenly, Uncle Mort realized something. He jumped to his feet from his chair. "Wait a second. Your cousin wasn't supposed to leave!"

"And who were those kids with him?" Gretel pointed out to her father.

"Oh, good job, Dad!" Gus quipped.

Uncle Mort nearly tripped over his feet as he ran to the front door. He grabbed the door handle and shouted out into the street for his nephew.

But it was too late. The three boys had already vanished into the night.

CHAPTER TWENTY-NINE

Time To Panic?

Marge was seated in her new office, taking in the atmosphere. She was ecstatic over her new surroundings, given to her by Mayor Norm Hull. She believed she earned her new title, even if it was a position given under unethical circumstances. She chuckled to herself and took a moment to congratulate herself.

"You're royal. You're royal, Marge. So much prettier than Eden, too!" Marge told herself as she smiled at her reflection in her computer's monitor.

The fantasy was short-lived, however, as her telephone on her desk roared to life, ruining the moment.

"Great! Who could that be? And at this hour, too?" Marge glanced at the clock on her wall. It was almost 9:30. The voice on the other end breathed heavily, almost startling her. She checked the ID readout on the phone's cradle. It was Mort, her loving husband.

"Marge, dear," Mort said desperately, out of breath. "We have trouble!"

"What kind of trouble?" Marge replied, unfazed, and began to work on other things. She wasn't even paying attention to Mort. She loved her husband deeply, but her new power as a highly ranked Dagger-Bagger was going to her head, quickly. She began to have a fantasy of the day she became Mayor of Harmony after Norm Hull became King of The Land of Fenton, permanently. She grinned. Mort, however, was beginning to annoy her with his constant calling lately.

Mort sighed, "Well, Gabriel was in his room. He walked out to watch the press conference. We laughed at him, and then he was back in his room, and then…"

Marge quickly cut him off, "Whoa, hon! Please! Just give me the meat of the story!"

Mort breathed out slowly as he tried to put his thoughts together concisely. He decided to sum up the words in one sentence, "Gabriel left the house!"

There was no reply on the other end of the line.

"Marge?" Mort croaked out.

Marge sighed heavily into the phone, clearly irritated, "I'm here, Mort. Is that the emergency?" She didn't want to appear weak, however.

Mort replied weakly, "Well, yes, but… he left… with two others!"

Marge sat up in her seat. She was now listening. She closed her game of solitaire on the computer screen. "Two older gentlemen?"

"I don't think so. Honestly, I didn't get a good look at them. I didn't even look. I only saw Gabriel's reflection in the television screen. I never look at the boy if I can help it, you know that," Mort replied weaker than ever.

"You had one job, Mort. I told you to keep him in that house until Mayor Hull and I figured out our plan!"

"I know, but…" Mort pleaded.

"Idiot!" Marge slammed down the phone.

Marge bolted from her office and hurried down the long corridor toward Mayor Hull's office. The door was shut. She knocked on it loudly. "Mayor Hull," she said before opening it.

Mayor Hull was seated at his desk counting money he'd stolen from various citizens while out campaigning. He always stole money from safes or wallets when citizens weren't paying attention. "Yes?" He replied, obviously annoyed he was being interrupted.

"Gabriel's already on his way here!" Marge shouted frantically.

"He is, is he?" Mayor Hull replied casually as he put down another bill. "Ten thousand and fourteen…"

"He's on his way here!" Marge cried out. After Norm Hull never even looked up, Marge realized her leader was far from discouraged about the matter. She tilted her head. It just didn't make any sense. "Why aren't you more worried about this matter?"

"So, you mean to tell me that you are worried?" Mayor Hull returned the same question to her with a smile.

Marge grew more and more frustrated. "Yes! The plan isn't even close to being fleshed out!"

As she frantically raised her concerns, Mayor Hull began to laugh.

"Why are you laughing, sir?" Marge demanded.

"Because this is the perfect opportunity to throw him further off course, Marge." Mayor Hull stood from his desk chair. He gathered his money and walked to his wall safe to put it away. He punched a few numbers as the safe opened and then loudly closed, securing the money inside.

Marge approached Mayor Hull and shook her head. "I don't understand," she replied, as she tried to piece together what he was trying to say.

Mayor Hull walked back to his desk and grabbed a remote from the drawer. He smiled again. "It may be easier to show you as I explain," he began.

CHAPTER THIRTY

Double Trouble

Gabriel walked slowly with Walter and Abram down Elm Street. They were careful to avoid any signs of Dagger-Baggers hidden in the shadows. As they walked down the long street, streetlights showed them the way toward the Harmony Municipal Building.

"This place still gives me the creeps!" Abram groaned. "Look at the way all the houses look exactly the same!"

Walter was experiencing some serious déjà vu with that comment but he nodded as he pushed his wire-rimmed glasses up on his face. "Yeah? Well how about the cars? All the same model. That's even creepier! Nothing has changed in over thirteen years!"

Gabriel listened to the two as they bickered back and forth and shook his head. He missed them both. Walter and Abram had been best friends for years and years. They were always trying to one-up the other.

"I missed you two so much," Gabriel smiled through his words.

"We missed you, too, Gabriel," Abram nodded.

Walter laughed, "We don't mean to bicker. It's how we show love, I suppose."

As they inched closer to their target, Harmony's Municipal Building, they spotted more Dagger-Baggers. They were quick to take an alternate route to stay out of sight. Gabriel believed somewhere inside the building they would find the oil canvas painting,

As the sight of the building became clearer and clearer to their view, Gabriel felt a small pebble hit him on the back of the head and then heard it fall to the ground below.

"Hey!" Gabriel cried out. "What was that?" He rubbed the back of his head to soothe the brief pain he felt.

Walter, Abram, and Gabriel turned around to see what caused the brief interruption of their warm reunion.

"Oh, no!" Gabriel gasped. He spotted the familiar sight and suddenly felt a greater pain than the pebble.

"Yo, Pea Brain!" the familiar face said to him.

Gabriel stared in horror to see his cousins on their bicycles staring back at him, smiling. Their big, coal-colored eyes made him swallow heavily in his throat.

"Hello, Cousin!" Gretel waved.

Marge and Mayor Hull searched through channels on a computer monitor, which gave a live feed of Harmony. From the monitor, Mayor Hull could see anything on the streets he wanted.

"When did you get this made?" Marge asked as she watched Mayor Hull scan channels.

"I had it installed while we were in The Land of Fenton this last time. It was strictly a security precaution, because I knew Gabriel would be a bigger threat to us! Only cost the tax payers a few extra million."

Marge smirked, "Shame. But smart thinking."

Mayor Hull searched until he landed on the channel that gave a view of Elm Street.

"There! That's the one!" Mayor Hull smiled. "Look what we have here!" He pushed his chair closer. "They found him!" He then rubbed his hands together excitedly.

Marge looked on as she saw her son, daughter, and nephew with two other boys. She smiled. "Oh, my children! I knew you'd come through for me!"

The plan was working perfectly. The Dagger-Baggers in training were doing just as they were told, Mayor Hull smiled as he looked on. "Wait a minute! Something's not right here!" Mayor Hull said as he tilted his head and zoomed in on the scene of the two boys that he didn't recognize.

Marge looked at her leader as if she thought the man was going crazy. "I don't understand, sir. What isn't right?"

The Mayor pointed to the screen, "Those two boys. There!" He looked at Marge for a long moment before continuing, "I make it my mission to learn all my voters in Harmony and their children, and I've never seen those two anywhere!"

Marge raised an eyebrow, "You don't mean…?"

"Exactly!" Mayor Hull scoffed. "They must be from The Land of Fenton!"

"But how?" Marge questioned. "We have the oil canvas painting! There's no way he went to get help. He couldn't have found it! The pirate ships were sunk during the battle back in The Land of Fenton. How did they get here?"

Mayor Hull clenched his right fist. "He has my brother and father's powers and your sister's pure heart. Marge, wake up! He's capable of anything!"

"He must be stopped before this gets further out of hand!" Marge said as she bit her bottom lip, causing blood to drip down to her chin.

CHAPTER THIRTY-ONE

The Empty House

Gus stared into the eyes of his cousin, Gabriel, for a long time, and Gabriel stared right back. Neither spoke during the staring contest. The only sounds heard were crickets in the grass and owls in the trees.

Gretel finally broke the silence by raising her finger to her lips, "Hush! We need to talk. Not here, however."

Gabriel turned to Gretel, confused, and tilted his head. "Huh?"

She gestured toward a pole at a camera that was pointed directly at them. "Cameras!" she replied with her teeth clenched.

Gabriel nodded, but still confused. "I don't…"

She cut him off, "Not another word." Her teeth still clenched.

The group was unaware they could only be seen and not heard.

Walter, Gabriel, and Abram watched as Gus and Gretel began slowly pedaling away on their bicycles back down Elm Street. They were heading in the opposite direction they were heading before, however. This direction wouldn't lead them toward Harmony's Municipal Building.

"Follow us," Gus insisted. "Trust us!"

Gabriel was unsure because his grandfather, King Shamus always taught him to follow his heart. At that moment, his heart was beating wildly. He clutched his chest, confused. "What would you do, Grandfather?" Gabriel whispered to himself.

Walter and Abram turned to Gabriel, as if they were looking for permission to follow the two. Gabriel decided it was in their best interest to follow them and took off toward his cousins.

"Let's go!" Gabriel instructed and the three followed Gus and Gretel to an unknown location.

The journey was long. Gabriel thought about his long walks in The Land of Fenton. There was plenty of beautiful sights to keep one interested, but here in Harmony, it was a struggle to keep up with Gus and Gretel. His cousins often looked back to make sure they were still being followed.

"Where are we going?" Gabriel asked about three miles into their journey, huffing and puffing as he jogged from behind.

"We're almost there," Gretel replied.

Walter and Abram began their usual back and forth bickering once again.

"I don't think this is a good idea," Abram grunted.

Walter rolled his eyes, "The boy knows more than you give him credit for, my friend!"

"It's obviously a trap," Abram continued, ignoring

Walter.

Gabriel hushed them as they reached a new street: Maple Avenue. This was an unfamiliar street for Gabriel, and he turned to Walter and Abram. He shrugged his shoulders when they asked where they were headed. "I don't know. Gus and Gretel are leading us, remember?" Gabriel said to them. "This is my first time out of the house."

Within a few minutes, Gretel and Gus put the brakes on their bicycles in front of an abandoned house.

"Here!" Gus said, and he and Gretel then continued onward up the driveway.

Gabriel stared at the house with a confused face. The shape was exactly the same as any other house in Harmony, but the house had lost its coloring long, long ago. The yard was also in desperate need of maintenance. It was covered in weeds and debris. Gabriel stood motionless for a moment as he studied all the decay surrounding the house.

Abram stood to Gabriel's right and Walter to his left.

"I don't think we should enter," Abram whispered.

Gabriel looked ahead as Gus pushed open the front door after a bit of a struggle.

Gretel, who was closer behind her brother, motioned for Gabriel to follow them. "Your friends, too," she said. "Come on!"

Walter nudged Gabriel with his elbow. "Go on, my boy. We're right behind you." But Walter stood there, waiting to be told to move. However, he told himself he would only move if the order came from Gabriel.

Abram shook his head with a gasp, "Are you nuts, Walter?" Go inside an abandoned house? In Harmony of all places?"

Walter nodded, "The boy has heart! He knows when to trust his instincts!"

Gabriel swallowed hard in his throat as he took a small step forward. His heart was once again beating wildly in his chest. "Was this the right move?" His heart slowed and he took another step forward as Walter and Abram slowly followed closely behind him, bickering with one another, yet again.

"We're coming!" Abram and Walter said in unison. He could hear the two of them whispering to one another.

Gabriel stepped inside the abandoned house with Walter and Gabriel clutching his shirt tightly, unaware of what they might find inside.

Mayor Hull pointed his remote at the monitor. He changed channel after channel after channel on his monitor and then let out a loud grunt. He banged his fist on his desk.

"I don't understand! Where are they?" Marge asked as she looked over his shoulder from behind his desk.

"There are cameras all over Harmony. Why am I not finding them on any of the channels?" Mayor Hull grunted again as he changed the channels again.

"Wait a minute!" Marge snapped her fingers. "Try that

abandoned neighborhood on Maple."

"Why would they go on Maple? It's been vacant for years!" Mayor Hull asked.

Marge sighed with an eye roll, "It's worth a shot!"

"Fine, whatever," Mayor Hull said as he turned the channels until he saw Gabriel and the two unknown boys walking inside an abandoned home. Mayor Hull smiled, "Seems I owe you an apology, Marge! What do we have here?"

"Zoom in toward that window!" Marge commanded as she pointed to the monitor. Mayor Hull zoomed in and Marge gasped, "That's my son and my daughter!" Marge pursed her lips, "Why are they there, too?"

"Isn't it obvious?" Mayor Hull replied.

Marge shook her head, "Let me guess. You're going to explain again?"

Mayor Hull smiled and winked at his deputy mayor. "Oh, you know me so well, Marge."

CHAPTER THIRTY-TWO

Hidden Roots

Surprisingly, the lights were still in working order inside the abandoned house. Gabriel looked around and searched for his cousins. He was half expecting one of them to pop out with a bigger, stronger Dagger-Bagger and haul him off to his Aunt Marge or his Uncle N.H. for another battle.

Fortunately, he found his cousins alone in the small living room. The place was in much need of a renovation. Gabriel spotted ratty, old furniture. Trash was everywhere. The house was outfitted just like the house he knew back on 3000 Elm Street, despite its decay. Gabriel feared the place was infested with rats, probably carrying harmful diseases. The Land of Fenton had many rats that were friendly. However, the rats back in Harmony were awful, terrifying creatures.

"Have a seat," Gus said in a much friendlier tone than he'd ever heard in the more than thirteen years he'd known him. His cousin pointed to the sofa. Gus himself was seated in a chair, and Gretel sat on the chair's arm.

Gabriel nodded, and Walter and Abram followed him toward the sofa. He was still unsure if this was the right idea but trusted his heart for now. "Have faith, Gabriel," he reminded himself under his breath.

Gretel spoke first after the three sat down. "First things first. Gabriel, who are your friends?"

Gabriel shifted in his seat after the question was posed. His pure heart didn't allow him to lie very easily. He just kept quiet for the moment.

Gretel's brother picked up where his sister left off, "Pea Brain, no one else is here. There are no cameras. Just tell us."

Gabriel sighed heavily and nodded, "Okay, fine." He was prepared to come clean. However, before he could speak, he turned to his right and then to his left. Suddenly, he saw Walter and Abram morph back into their previous bodies. Gabriel's jaw dropped. He was prepared for the worst when he looked back at Gus and Gretel's faces. They both looked shocked beyond belief.

"My name is Abram. I am the Legendary Wizard from The Land of Fenton, and your cousin's godfather," Abram said bravely. He smiled and showed no signs of fear.

Walter cleared his throat, looking straight into the eyes of Gabriel's cousins. He didn't blink as he spoke, "I am the Great Warrior known as Walter, Gabriel's caretaker. I'm older than anyone in this room, put together."

Gus and Gretel were still shocked over the events that had unfolded before them. For a moment, Gabriel didn't know what to think. He felt a lump in his throat begin to form as Gus stood from the chair and made his way toward them. He saw his cousin standing above him. Gus stuck his hand out in front of him, and Gabriel closed his eyes.

"Please don't hurt me!" Gabriel cried out. He never felt this kind of fear back in The Land of Fenton, so why was it any different in Harmony?

"I'm sorry," Gus said softly.

A long silence followed with Gabriel's eyes still shut tightly before he finally opened them, "You're what?" Gabriel uttered.

Gretel stood from the arm of the chair and walked behind her cousin, touching his shoulder. She whispered, "It's true, Gabriel. We're both sorry."

Gus tried again, "I'm sorry, Pea Brain."

Gabriel studied his cousin's hand. He realized he was not trying to hurt him but only wanted to shake his hand.

"I don't understand," Gabriel said, still not shaking his cousin's hand.

Gretel started the story, "Well, this all started right before Mom's press conference. We realized how evil she'd been and was trying to become. I decided to renounce my training and status as a Dagger-Bagger. I told Gus, and he agreed to do the same. But then…"

Gus started to speak again, "Then something weird began to happen to my sister."

"What happened?" Gabriel asked.

"It's best if we show instead of tell you," Gretel said. The two then left the room.

For several minutes, Gabriel, Walter, and Abram were left alone in the living room. They whispered their confusion to one another while Gus and Gretel were off in another room and making a lot of noise. Gabriel heard running water and noises of pots and pans crashing from the other room. Walter and Abram jumped at the noise.

"Sorry, we dropped a pot, and it caused an avalanche!" Gus called out from the kitchen.

Soon after, Gretel returned with Gus carrying a big bowl filled with water. Gretel was carrying a washcloth. She had a look of fear in her eyes.

"What's that for, Gretel?" Gabriel asked, pointing to the items.

"Just watch!" Gretel said, hushing him. She then sat the bowl on top of the coffee table, took the washcloth, and dipped it inside the bowl.

Gabriel was not sure what his cousin was doing. Were they about to wash each other's feet? He read about that in the big book back in The Land of Fenton.

"Watch closely," Gretel said. She then took the washcloth and began scrubbing the scalp of her hair. Gabriel found this very strange. Suddenly, after a few moments she bent forward to show the results to her cousin.

Gabriel looked at Gretel's hair on her head. What had once been covered in brown hair was now showing small patches of blond hair! Gabriel's eyes grew wide as he gasped, "Oh, my goodness! Gretel, your hair is blond!"

Gretel nodded and a small tear fell down from her right eye. "I noticed it the morning after Gus and I decided to no longer be Dagger-Baggers!"

Gabriel turned his attention to Gus now, "Did your hair begin to turn blond, too?"

"No, not yet," Gus replied. He quickly shrugged it off.

"And not everyone will ever have blond hair," Abram explained softly. "That doesn't mean you're a bad person."

Gabriel then watched Gretel frantically dig into a nearby bag from her chair. "Sorry, I have to take care of this!"

"Take care of what?" Gabriel asked, taking a step back in fear from her dramatic antics.

"This!" Gretel said pointing to her hair. She spoke like a scared child who had just done something wrong. She continued to frantically dig deeper, deeper into the bag. Gretel finally retrieved what she was looking for and began applying dark colors of makeup and other dark, putty-like items to her hair. She used this to cover up the blond patches. After a few minutes, the blond was hidden once again.

Gabriel stared at his cousin and frowned, "I wish you didn't have to do that." His heart began to ache.

His cousin nodded. "Well, I do, too. However, if I'm caught with blond hair, you know what will happen to me. I will be banished forever! Harmony only allows sameness. They may have lifted the two-child policy, but blond children are still not allowed. I will be kicked out forever! Who knows what will happen to me?!" Gretel began to cry again.

It was then Gabriel realized he may be doomed to be captured eventually. He ran a hand through his thick blond hair, nervously. He had to make his way back to The Land of Fenton and quickly!

Walter and Abram stared at Gretel. Their eyes showed hurt for the young girl, "Well, it's a pleasure to have you on our side," Abram said gently. He rose to his feet to hug her.

"Absolutely. Gretel, our differences are what make each person special," Walter echoed. "We were created to be different. Our power and love pales in comparison to the Creator. He loves you, just the way you are, Gretel." Walter patted Gretel's shoulder, soothingly.

Gretel smiled genuinely, still in tears. "Thank you, but now we just need to find a way to take down the evil dynamic duo."

Her brother turned to her and touched her shoulder. "Don't worry, Sis. I have a plan."

CHAPTER THIRTY-THREE

The Plan

Mayor Hull zoomed in through the window to show the group smiling. They could see Gabriel, Gus, Gretel, and the backs of two others. He couldn't make out who they were, however. He assumed they were the same two boys from earlier.

"I still don't understand. I thought you were going to explain this to me," Marge said with a shake of her head.

The Mayor shook his head. "Marge, I'm afraid your daughter and son may have switched sides."

Marge suddenly pushed Mayor Hull's chair out of the way while he was still sitting in it. "What?" Marge roared loudly as she slammed her hand down on his desk. "How can this be?"

Mayor Hull breathed out through his nose. "Look, I already told you that they were supposed to bring them here to us, right? The plan was for our Dagger-Baggers to not even try to capture them if they saw him on the streets. We made Gabriel think he could just walk in here. We gave him a false sense of security with your son and daughter. Well, if they didn't bring them here, it appears they chose good over evil. Your son and daughter being the good, unfortunately."

Marge's skinny face sunk in tighter as she heard the words Mayor Hull spoke, "Why would you choose good over evil?"

Mayor Hull rolled his chair back to his desk, "Calm down! We can still beat Gabriel. It appears blood isn't always thicker than water, but we are smarter than they are, Marge! Remember that!"

Marge nodded but sighed, "So, what do you propose we do now?"

"The plan is already in motion, my dear. There are many, many ways to get through to a naïve Dagger-Bagger. I thought of one already. And it worked." Mayor Hull laughed, as he looked at his wall safe.

The others listened intently as Gus explained his plan in detail. According to Gus, the best way to take down Marge was through her husband. Abram was to be the leader in the effort, Gus reiterated.

"So, how does that involve me?" Abram questioned again.

"You are going to use magic to impersonate my father. Just like you did earlier!" Gus replied with a smile.

Walter stood up and shook his head. He began to wave his hands back and forth. "Nope. No. Absolutely not!" He continued to wave his hands back and forth.

Gabriel watched Abram smile at the idea of using magic in Harmony yet again. He knew that Abram was much looser about the idea of using magic outside The Land of Fenton.

"Oh, come on, Walter!" Abram begged. "Please!"

Walter shook his head, "It's out of the question, and you know why! Besides you promised!"

Abram rolled his eyes, "You are such a bore. Always saying we should only use it when absolutely necessary. But this is a pretty important time, don't you think?" He groaned. "I seem to recall a time when…"

Walter cut him off, "Fine! But be careful! If we are caught impersonating a Dagger-Bagger, you know the consequences!"

Abram nodded and did a victory dance for winning the debate. He then pulled Walter in for a tight hug. "Thanks, old man!"

Gabriel stood up. "Whoa! Whoa! Wait! What's the consequence for impersonating a Dagger-Bagger?"

Walter adjusted his shiny robe and looked at Abram in annoyance over the hug. "Well, for starters, you lose all your magical power."

Gabriel gasped. "Well, that's not good!"

Walter cleared his throat after being interrupted. "Gabriel, that's not all."

Abram sighed and rolled his eyes. He felt Walter was overreacting. "Walter, come on, you're being paranoid!"

"May I continue, please?" Walter asked as he looked at Abram, still annoyed. "You also are banished from The Land of Fenton for forever. Next, you become a Dagger-Bagger yourself and are sent to live in Harmony. It's considered an abuse of magic!"

Gabriel swallowed heavily in his throat, instantly regretting asking. He didn't know how to reply. "Well, I guess you better be careful then, Abram." He felt his heart begin to beat wildly in his chest. Maybe this was a bad idea, after all.

Gus continued explaining the plan. "Okay, Abram, you will also need to make sure you sound like my father, or our entire plan will be a failure."

"Check!" Abram replied excitedly. He could not sit still.

"So, what is he going to do with Mom, anyway?" Gretel asked.

"Well, tomorrow is Mom and Dad's anniversary. Abram will keep Mom distracted in her office while the rest of us try to lure Mayor Hull back to The Land of Fenton for Gabriel," Gus explained.

Walter interjected. He felt this plan was a waste of time, "What about your actual father, Gus? What if he shows up?"

Gus smiled, "Great thinking! I thought about that, too, Walter. That's where you come in, Gretel!"

Gretel watched as Gus tossed her a bottle of cough syrup. "I don't understand."

"You're going to be sick, and Daddy's going to take care of you."

Gretel smiled. "So, we won't give him a chance to leave the house then, right?"

Gus nodded, "Exactly! Bingo!"

Walter sat down again, dumfounded. Gus actually came up with a plan that made sense. While he did have questions, he had to hand it to the boy. "I'm in."

The group went over a few more details for a little longer. They discussed how they would have to enter from the alleyway through the basement at Harmony's Municipal Building, but Abram could enter through the front door once he assumed his Mort disguise. Once inside, they would be able to use magic, if necessary and knock out any Dagger-Baggers.

Gabriel's hope was for Marge to give up the information on where the oil canvas painting was located. He was sure it was located at Harmony's Municipal

Building. He smiled to himself. His cousin's plan was crazy. Yes, it was crazy enough that it might actually work.

CHAPTER THIRTY-FOUR

The (Not So) Sick Child

The next afternoon, the cousins and Walter and Abram walked out of the house and down the driveway. Gus and Gretel decided it would be best for everyone to travel by foot, so they left their bicycles behind. Gretel would walk as far down Maple Avenue as she could but knew she would have to soon turn on to Elm Street for her part in the plan. Walter was coaching her with convincing techniques on how to appear sickly.

"I am over one hundred years old. I have had more colds than the number of days you have been alive!" Walter chuckled.

Only the night before, Gretel and Gus snuck into the house at 3000 Elm Street to grab a few items. Gretel never said what her item was, only that she used a combination lock to retrieve it.

"All will be revealed in good time, Gabriel," Gretel said with a beaming smile.

Gus, however, grabbed several watches from his Dad's collection. Finally, Mort's career as a watch and jewelry salesman paid off. Gus said he would pass the watches out later.

Walter cleared his throat, trying to bring his focus back to feigning sickness. Gretel nodded and produced several coughing fits.

"Good! That was better," Walter said as he smiled.

Gretel groaned loudly, "Ugh! Can't you just cast a temporary spell on me and make me look sick?" Gretel begged the old man.

"I'm afraid my magic doesn't work that way," Walter laughed softly.

Abram interjected quickly, "Besides, you know he won't do magic unless…"

Walter cut him off. "Enough, Abram!"

At the end of the street, Gretel turned to the group with a heavy sigh, "Well, this is where our paths change."

She hugged each of them goodbye and turned to walk down Elm Street where her father would be waiting. She hoped Mort's pea-sized brain would fall for her brother's extremely complicated plan.

Marge busied herself at her desk. Her job as deputy mayor wasn't a busy one. However, her job trying to figure out the best way to take down her nephew was a full-time one. She scrambled to come up with the best strategy for doing just that. As such, she had no clue what day it was or if it held any significance.

This, however, was not the case for her husband, Mort. He was spending his entire morning focusing on how he might surprise his wife of sixteen years. He spent the entire morning polishing a diamond necklace he recently acquired from one of his suppliers. He wanted to take Marge's breath away with the extravagant gift. It was rare for Mort to spend money but never when it came to his wife. He was, after all, still in the doghouse for losing track of his nephew by letting him out of their home.

Mort began to pace back and forth in his bedroom as he tried to pick out the best outfit to wear. "Just relax, old man. You can do this!" He settled on a suit he last wore ten years ago. It was faded and worn out, just like Mort.

He straightened his mismatched tie as he looked in the mirror. "Just get dressed, then head out to her office and knock her dead with your good looks!" He still looked sloppily dressed as he reached to grab his shoes from his closet. Before Mort could tie his shoes, he heard the front door open and close again.

"Daddy?" a voice called out weakly.

Mort ran toward the voice. His shoestrings dangled on the floor causing him to trip and fall. He quickly picked himself up again. "Gretel?" Mort asked, looking concerned, as Gretel began coughing, uncontrollably once he spotted her.

"Daddy, I'm sick!" Gretel uttered. She coughed three more times and began to look paler in color by the second. She began to shake a little, too.

Mort rushed to his daughter's side, still clutching his wife's precious diamond necklace in his right hand. He then slipped the expensive gift into his pocket and sighed dramatically.

"Oh, sweetie," Mort said almost tenderly. He always hated this part of being a parent. Things like this got in the way of other plans.

"Daddy, were you going somewhere?" Gretel asked and then forced herself to have another coughing fit.

Mort touched the back of Gretel's head to soothe her. "Umm..."

"Could you maybe fix me a bowl of ice cream?" Gretel asked as she looked at him.

Her father nodded. He mentally kicked himself for agreeing.

"And a bowl of chicken noodle soup?" Gretel added.

Her father nodded again. Another mental kick.

It was at that moment Mort realized he was going to be spending his anniversary with a very sick and demanding child. His anniversary plans were now over.

He turned his back and headed for the kitchen to begin working on his demanding child's list.

Although Mort didn't see it, his daughter smiled.

CHAPTER THIRTY-FIVE

Abram's Memory

As Abram walked along with Gus, Walter and Gabriel, he was reminded of his past with Marge Canton. He knew her when she was quite young. He was all too familiar with her wicked ways and knew it was going to be difficult to pretend to be her husband, Mort. He knew Marge when she was a student at Fenton Academy. He knew Marge when her eyes were still blue…

A voice shouted loudly as a bell rang out, "Marge!"

She was always late to class, unlike her perfect sister, Eden. She never had a valid excuse for being late either.

Punctuality was not on her to-do list. Her father, Gabriel, but everyone called, Gabe, was not proud of this and told her to try to be more like her sister.

"Sorry, Abram, my mistake!" Marge replied with a phony smile as she walked into the crowded classroom. She proceeded to take her seat in the back. She would often prop her feet up on the chair in front of her. Today was one of those days.

A classmate groaned at her feet being on his back, "Stop it!" he called out in Marge's direction.

"Marge!" Abram cleared his throat.

Marge rolled her eyes and shoved her feet to the floor, "Sorry again, Abram." She wasn't sorry, however. Coming to class was a chore and she hated doing chores. She knew if she ever found a husband, she'd never be a housewife.

Abram continued his lecture with the class. His lessons the last few weeks were focused on being kind to the environment. The Land of Fenton was free from threats of environmental destruction and prided itself on this factor.

There were oceans of blue and green colors and forests of natural wonder. The colors made for beautiful post cards of how life was precious, no matter the form. All the animals and humans lived in perfect harmony. There were people of all races living together. The Land of Fenton was a place for people of all backgrounds. The people of The Land of Fenton embraced differences. They believed in a Creator who provided them with the opportunity to live in a World that was nearly perfect. None of the citizens wanted to ruin it. The environment continued to thrive because people were kind to it, and in doing so, the people living in it, thrived, too.

However, pirates that lived on the outskirts of The Land of Fenton, often threatened this tranquility. This place was known as Harmony and not much was known about it unless you had a pirate ship to visit firsthand. No other magic was known on how to see Harmony firsthand. Not that a Wizard would want to visit there, anyhow. Usually only banished beings went there. So, Abram felt the need to stress the need for being kind to the environment and explain how good conquers evil.

For homework the night before, Abram asked his students to provide spells to help the environment defend itself for generations. He particularly hoped the students would focus on animals. Eden, as usual, was the first to volunteer to present her spell.

The pale, blue-eyed ten-year-old stepped up to the front and smiled. Waiting for her to speak, the class was all smile. She had many, many friends. "Abram, I knew in my heart this would be the perfect assignment for me as I honestly feel this could be my gift. I have a love for animals, and I think it would be great if animals could speak to us."

This had never been attempted before so there was quite a bit of skepticism among the group. There was a soft murmur in the crowded room. None in the room were skeptical of her potential, however. Except for maybe one.

Abram nodded, "I see. How do you mean?"

"Well, I have come up with a spell that will allow animals to speak. I will now test it out on my pet rabbit."

Eden then walked across the classroom to pull out a beautiful white rabbit from a cage. She walked back to the middle of the room and put the rabbit on a wooden stool. She then recited a spell. When she was finished, she spoke directly to the rabbit with a big grin. "Hello, Jasper!"

The beautiful, fluffy, white rabbit sniffed the air and looked around at the students. He looked frightened for a moment, but then he stood on his two back legs. Suddenly, he clicked his teeth, "Hello, Eden!"

The class gasped and began to clap loudly, but Eden held up her hand, "Quiet, please! Don't scare him!" The class was hushed almost instantly. Eden smiled and continued, "Can you tell us what it's like to be a rabbit, Jasper?"

Jasper appeared to ponder the question for a moment. He even tilted his head, "Well, I really love being a rabbit, but I don't like my silly, tiny cage. I really prefer Faith Park where I can play with other rabbits. Oh, and I like to go there to play with you."

The class was all smiles except for Marge. She rolled her eyes. "Oh, give me a break!" she uttered.

Abram looked over at Marge and raised an eyebrow, "Something the matter, Marge?" he asked.

"Yes, something is the matter! My perfect sister is wowing the class once again with something that won't solve anything!" Marge groaned.

"If you'd like to give a rebuttal you can, Marge," Eden replied as she fed some clover to Jasper.

"Well, how is that spell going to help the environment? How is this going to help animals?" Marge asked in a testy, antagonistic manner.

Eden gently replied, "Well, I think with them being able to speak, it will help us better understand their needs. This will bridge the gap between human and animal!"

Abram adjusted his multi-colored robe before walking over to Marge's desk. "Young lady, your sister has just achieved something remarkable. She has created a spell to teach animals to speak. This has never been done before!"

Marge folded her fingers over her thumb to make a flapping gesture. "Blah, blah, blah, blah!"

"Marge! One more comment like that and you will be kicked out of my class!" Abram said as he tapped Marge's desk with his Wizard wand.

"Please! You always say that, and you never do it." Marge said with a laugh. "Do it. I dare you!" Her eyes burned into Abram's soul.

Abram pursed his lips. His heart began to ache. "King Shamus would be so hurt to know how you are acting, Marge." He felt his lip tremble. However, he knew he couldn't cry in front of his students.

"Marge, please! Daddy wouldn't like…" Eden begged.

Marge got up from her seat and walked up to the front of the room. "What's this?" she asked as she spotted something next to Eden's spell book.

"Oh, um, please don't do anything with that!" Eden cried out.

Marge grabbed it as Eden tried to take it from her. However, Marge pushed her away, knocking Eden on to the floor. Some students rushed to help Eden up.

"Oh, it's a spell reversal!" Marge said with an evil smile.

Eden climbed to her feet, but it was too late. Marge was already reading the spell reversal.

"Jasper!" Eden frantically yelled.

The class waited and waited but Jasper did not speak back to Eden. He was unable to speak.

Abram was suddenly red-faced and looked over at a smiling and laughing Marge. His anger reached its climax. "Get out of my class, Marge!"

Marge nodded, still clutching the spell reversal. "I'll go, but I'm taking this with me!" she said as she held the spell reversal. "Sister, you may be able to teach them to speak, but I will always be right behind you to undo what you have done!"

Abram opened the classroom door and watched Marge leave. He heard her laughing all the way down the hall. He took Eden by the side to apologize for everything. He told her to never give up on her spell to teach animals to speak. "Be sure to work with King Shamus because there is safety in numbers," Abram explained. "I know he will be very impressed with your talents."

Eden shook her head, "I don't know King Shamus, Abram."

"But I do," Abram smiled. "He's my employer outside of the school."

Although she had to continue going to school, this remarkable incident paved the way for Eden to meet King Shamus. It also led to the meeting of her future husband, Matthew. On the other side, however, it also paved the way to the eventual banishment of Marge.

Abram was still haunted by the memory of that day because he felt he gave up on Marge too quickly. She must have taught other Dagger-Baggers the reversal spell. Although Abram wasn't to blame for Marge's banishment, he still didn't rest easy for all those years when he thought of that memory. Eden was able to teach more animals to speak than Marge was able to reverse, but it still didn't help with Abram's guilt. Maybe he should have worked harder to teach goodness to her. Maybe it would have helped.

Walter nudged his friend, Abram. "Hey, are you okay?"

Abram simply nodded. "Yeah. Just a lot on my mind as I prepare to do this charade later."

"That's what you get for volunteering, my friend," Walter whispered. "I tried to tell you this was a bad idea."

Abram didn't want to admit it, but he feared his friend might be right.

Finally, when the group was less than half a mile from Harmony's Municipal Building, Gabriel turned toward Abram. "Are you ready?"

Walter turned toward his life-long friend. Abram sighed and nodded. "I hope so. I suppose it's now or never."

The two long-time friends put their hands together and began to recite the spell.

Gabriel and Gus looked on with amazement as Abram slowly began to morph into Mort Canton.

CHAPTER THIRTY-SIX

Gabriel's Vision

Gabriel, Gus, and Walter continued to make their way toward Harmony's Municipal Building. It was now late afternoon, and the sun was beating down heavily. It was an unusually hot day. Once they reached their location, they quickly spotted several Dagger-Baggers out front. Each looked more intimidating than the next. The Dagger-Baggers were armed with bows and arrows. Abram, in his Mort disguise, made his way to the front doors. He was stopped by Gus, as he had something to give him. He knew he had no reason to fear the Dagger-Baggers in his present state.

Gus, Gabriel, and Walter waited until the right moment before sneaking around to the alleyway nearby.

They knew if they were caught, their plan would be over, especially for Gabriel and Walter.

At this moment, Gus began to pass out the other item that was retrieved the night before. He gave each a special watch containing a two-way radio with private channels. It was one of the few gadgets he sold that worked. Gus said they would help them in their journey. He, however, did not give one to Gretel earlier.

"She can just text me if we need her," Gus explained. He also knew that if Gretel had a watch, Mort would be suspicious. The watches would be more discreet at Harmony's Municipal Building for the four of them. Gus further explained this would allow them to stay in constant communication with one another while they looked for their three targets: Marge, Norm Hull, and, of course: the oil canvas painting.

Looking ahead, the two began to move closer toward their destination but were careful with each step made. As Gus, Walter, and Gabriel maneuvered their way through the alleyways, Abram moved to the front door.

Suddenly, as the group walked toward the alley, Gabriel stopped in his tracks. He couldn't move any further! His feet wouldn't move. He watched Walter and Gus continue on, but he wasn't able to do so himself. "What's going on?" Gabriel asked himself.

Then, he heard a voice that seemed to come out of nowhere. "Be careful!" The voice was loud and commanding.

"Gabriel looked to the right, and then to the left. He looked behind but didn't see anything there either. His feet were still glued to the ground. "Okay, who said that?" Gabriel asked, his voice a bit shaky. However, his heart remained calm.

There was no reply, and Gabriel was still unable to move. "Listen to your heart. Trust your instincts!" Gabriel heard the voice command.

Gabriel realized whose voice it was that time and looked up at the sky. "Grandfather?" he asked. There was a soft rumble of thunder heard in the distance.

As he looked up, Gabriel saw the clouds move in front of the afternoon sun to form into a silhouette of King Shamus, The Frog King.

"Be careful of those you think you trust, Gabriel!" King Shamus instructed. "Trust your instincts. Remember, you have the heart to know the difference."

Gabriel nodded. He was in such amazement over seeing his grandfather again but didn't know what to say. What could he say? Was this a time for chit-chat?

"Grandfather! Wait!" Then, before he could say anything more, the clouds separated, and the sun returned. Gabriel quickly shielded his eyes. He felt blinded by the rays of sunshine.

Gabriel tried to move again, and this time he was successful. He heard another voice this time. It was his cousin, Gus. "Hey, are you coming, Pea Brain?"

Gabriel took off running. "Yeah. Sorry!" He wondered why his cousin still called him that.

He watched as his cousin pointed toward an open window that seemed to lead into a basement. "I think this is our best bet to get inside," Gus said.

"Whatever you think is best," Gabriel said softly.

"Good," Gus smiled. He gave his cousin a wink.

Suddenly, Gabriel's heart began to feel differently than before. Was it the wink that set him off? He shrugged it off but continued to study his cousin's expression.

"That's weird," Gabriel thought. But he followed his cousin through the basement window and down into the darkness.

His heart, however, continued to beat wildly in his chest.

CHAPTER THIRTY-SEVEN

Trapped Below

Abram reached the second floor of Harmony's Municipal Building and looked for the elected officials' offices. He scanned the directory looking for the right one. "Come on! Come on! You have to be here somewhere!" Abram said as he looked for Marge's office.

"Hello, Mort!" a voice called out. Abram froze and turned around. His eyes grew wide as he saw Mayor Hull standing next to him.

"Oh, hello, Mr. Mayor. How are you?" Abram cleared his throat, remaining as calm as possible.

"Doing fine." The two shook hands. "I assume you are here to see your lovely wife, huh?" Mayor Hull gave him a cheesy, phony, politician's smile.

Abram nodded. "I am. I just seem to be turned around. Could you point me in the direction to her office?"

Mayor Hull laughed, "Certainly." Mayor Hull gave a few directions to Abram and patted him on the back. "Wonderful to see you again. Please let me know if you need anything."

Abram nodded. "Thanks again. I also appreciate you giving my wife such a great job."

The Mayor shrugged, "What can I say? It was much, much deserved. Oh, and please say hello to that wonderful daughter of yours for me." Mayor Hull gave Abram a playful wink.

Abram swallowed hard in his throat. Did he know? Did he know that the real Mort was back home with Gretel? Or was it just a coincidence? Why wouldn't he ask about Gus? Abram kept walking and didn't look back. He soon arrived at Marge's office. He breathed out slowly before knocking. He did a quick spell after making sure no one was looking and produced a bouquet of flowers in his hand.

"Well, here we go!" Abram said with a heavy sigh. Abram reached out to knock on the door.

Gabriel landed on both feet with a loud thud as he reached the basement floor. He knew this was the best way inside to ensure they didn't get caught but was still skeptical after hearing the warning from King Shamus a few moments before. Then his heart had that weird feeling. And what was up with that wink from Gus?

Walter was next and seemed to have no trouble at all despite his age to squeeze through the tiny window and jump to his feet down into the dark basement.

"You amaze me, Walter," Gabriel said softly as the two looked around the basement floor.

Walter smiled, "You underestimate me, my boy."

The two surveyed their surroundings for a moment before Gus spoke up. "We should probably split up. Maybe I'll go to your uncle's office, and you two go to my mom's office and check on Abram."

"Okay," Gabriel said as he tried to follow Gus toward the stairs.

Gus stood in Gabriel's way. "No, no! You guys take the service elevator. It's over there some place." He pointed to the left side of the room. "I will take the stairs."

Walter tilted his head, "Um, why?"

"Trust me, okay? If we go together, it'll look more suspicious" Gus smiled and winked again.

Gabriel's heart began to beat weirdly. There it was again. The wink. What was up with his heart? "Alright, you're right. Let's split up," Gabriel said.

Walter and Gabriel headed for the service elevator as Gus walked up the stairs. They found no service elevator.

Then a light turned on for a brief moment, and then off moments later from above. Gabriel heard a wicked laugh cry out. He and Walter turned around to see Gus at the top of the stairs holding a key. He heard Gus laugh again.

"What's so funny?" Gabriel asked.

"This was all too easy, Gabriel! Poor, Gretel! She's such a dumb blond!" Gus said as he took one step down the stairs. "She's even dumber than you, Pea Brain!" He took another step, "It's not her fault. She somehow decided that having a heart was better than having brains."

Gabriel suddenly realized what his Grandfather and his heart were trying to tell him. "But why?" he tilted his head in shock.

"Well, it all started when my sister decided to take after you! I went along with it because I knew I could fool her. Plus, it helped me lure you here. Mayor Hull is offering me a handsome cash reward for bringing you here." Gus snickered.

Walter pursed his lips and tightened his robe. "So, this is all because of money?"

Gus shook his head, "Not just money. There's power, too! I will become a full-fledged Dagger-Bagger after this! Usually you become a Dagger-Bagger when you are eighteen. Not me!"

"But you won't be able to use any of your power here!" Gabriel pointed out.

Gus shrugged, "I will once I get to the oil canvas painting. But wait, you don't know where it is. Do you, Pea Brain?"

Walter and Gabriel began rushing toward the stairs, but they were quickly blocked with a swift kick to the stomach by Gus. "Stay back!" Gus continued up the stairs again and opened the door to the basement after unlocking the door with his key. He clicked his teeth. "Oh, as you might have guessed, there is no service elevator. Sorry!"

Gus then smiled at them, raised his wrist and ripped off his watch and threw it down the stairs where it broke into several pieces. "I don't think you will be making it upstairs any time soon."

Walter shook his head, "You will be stopped. We won't give up!"

Gus rolled his eyes, "Try if you want. But this time, I have a key. The master key to every room in the building, too! Funny, how things change. Now, if you will excuse me, I have to warn my mother and Mayor Hull about the Mort imposter!"

Gabriel and Walter huddled together and watched in horror as the door slammed and locked behind them, trapping them inside.

CHAPTER THIRTY-EIGHT

Daddy's Little Girl

It all made sense to Gabriel now. Gretel's hair was beginning to change to blond, but Gus made the comment the hairs on his head were just slower to change. Gabriel felt like such a fool. He kicked himself mentally.

"I guess that's it," Gabriel said, feeling a single tear fall down his right cheek.

Walter looked at Gabriel. He wanted so badly to make the tears go away. Although, it was his job to take care of Gabriel, this was one area he was unable to fix things: pain. That was Abram's domain. Walter couldn't make tears go away.

"No, Gabriel. It's not over. We have to get up there before he gets to Abram!" Walter said in an authoritative voice.

Gabriel thought back to all of the training Abram gave him. He then remembered a spell that might actually work.

He wiped a tear away with his sleeve. "You are right, Walter. And I think I may know of a spell that can get us out of this place, too!"

Walter smiled, "Atta, boy! What is it?"

Gabriel snickered knowing his caretaker's heart. "Well, don't forget you promised you'd go along with doing magic no matter what as long as it would help us, right?"

Walter groaned, submitting, "I already agreed! What is it, my boy?"

Gabriel continued, "Well, do you remember the spell Abram taught me where we can turn invisible and then walk through walls for up to five minutes at a time?"

Walter smiled, "That sounds like it could work!" He then nodded, "See! I told you it wasn't over!"

"I guess I should have known to never question you," Gabriel replied. The two then discussed how they were going to put the plan into motion.

Gretel was on the sofa in the living room with a big bowl of chicken noodle soup propped up on her lap. She had an empty bowl of ice cream on the coffee table in front of her as well. Mort then walked in with a warm washcloth.

"What's that for, Daddy?" Gretel asked, turning down the television.

"It'll bring down that fever of yours," Mort replied. He placed it on her forehead, pushing it into her hair a little.

Gretel nodded. "Thanks, Daddy." She coughed a few times to keep up her charade and ate her soup. Once her father was out of the room, she pulled out her cell phone from under her blanket. "Any update?" Gretel typed in a text message to her brother. There was no immediate response, however.

After not getting a reply for a few minutes, she put her phone away and watched television. She ate her soup and felt her eyelids get heavier. Suddenly, she felt a presence in the room and woke up. Her father was towering over her.

"Daddy! You scared me!" Gretel croaked.

"I'm sorry, Gretel," Mort smiled. "I thought you might want a new washcloth. You've been asleep for almost an hour." Mort stepped up to her and sat on the edge of the sofa and removed the now-cold washcloth.

Gretel sighed as she sat up from the sofa. After her father removed the washcloth, she watched his warm expression change. His brow furrowed, and he looked at her with a face that seemed stricken with fear. His dark eyes were bursting with disgust and rage. They appeared to be filled with blood, too. "Um, Daddy? What's wrong?" Gretel nearly cried out.

Mort was motionless, unable to speak for a moment.

Gretel poked her father's kneecap with her index finger. "Daddy?"

Mort finally spoke and grabbed hold of Gretel's wrist after she poked him. "Get out of my house!" Mort hissed. His eyes were growing with an even greater rage.

Gretel stared at her father in fear. "Stop! Daddy! You're hurting me!" She rose to her feet with her father's grip getting tighter. As she stood up, the chicken noodle soup bowl fell on to the floor below nearly spilling on her feet. She stepped back just in time to avoid injury. On the back wall in the living room she caught a glimpse of herself in a mirror. She suddenly realized that the washcloth had removed her artificial brown hair coloring. Her new blond hair was now visible. "Oh, no!" Gretel cried out.

Mort loosened his grip on his daughter after seeing the fear in his daughter's eyes. "Get out of here!"

Gretel was unsure if her father was setting a trap. She quickly uttered, "No!"

Mort wasn't kidding around. "Did you misunderstand, Gretel? I said, 'Get out of here!'"

The daughter stared at her father. She felt sick, and this time, however, she wasn't faking it. "But, Daddy…" Gretel began.

"I will give you one more chance. Get out of here!" Mort commanded.

Gretel quickly nodded as she slipped out from his grip. "Okay!" She backed away from her father and walked toward the door.

Mort cleared his throat as Gretel grabbed hold of the door handle. "Oh, but Gretel, your mother won't go as easy on you."

His daughter looked at her father with growing fear.

"I'm giving you a head start." Mort smiled and pulled out his phone. "One… two…"

Gretel opened the door handle and ran out the front door and into the street, barely having time to grab her shoes next to the doormat.

CHAPTER THIRTY-NINE

Location Verified

Walter and Gabriel recited the spell together as they stood at the top of the stairs from inside the basement. "Here we go!" Walter squealed.

Gabriel could sense Walter's love for magic really coming through as their physical forms slowly dissolved before his eyes. "Whoa! So cool! Why didn't we just do this the first time?" Gabriel asked excitedly.

The two slipped through the door quickly and spotted several Dagger-Baggers. Gabriel held in a laugh.

"Perfect!" Gabriel said a bit too excitedly.

"Hush, Gabriel!" whispered Walter. "We don't want them to hear us. We need to find Gus and locate that key."

Walter moved with Gabriel toward the second floor. They continued their search for Gus and then spotted him whistling to himself, still clutching the key in his hand.

"Target found!" Gabriel said softly. "Let's get him!"

The two moved toward him, careful not to make a sound unless absolutely necessary.

"You remember the plan, right?" Gabriel whispered. "We take the key from his hand and then push him into a closet before he realizes what's going on."

They watched Gus for a few moments. They took quiet steps along the floor. Gus hummed to himself as he walked, and Gabriel and Walter inched closer and closer. For a moment, they thought they were caught when Gus turned back to look. Seeing nothing, he continued on his way toward Mayor Hull's office. Gabriel reached out nearly touching the key but missed. Walter pointed to a small custodian's closet.

"Now!" Gabriel said. This time, when he reached for the key, he was successful.

"Hey!" Gus cried out. "What's going on?"

Walter used his warrior skills and pushed him quickly into the custodian's closet after Gabriel unlocked it. Gabriel recited a quick spell that caused the room to be soundproof. "Just in case!" Gabriel smiled.

Walter pulled the door shut and Gabriel locked it.

"We can't leave him here," Walter said softly. "He may be evil, but we aren't evil, Gabriel!"

Gabriel shook his head. "Oh, I won't. We'll find a way to let him out. But first, we need to get our hands on the oil canvas painting!"

The two smiled at one another at having one less thing (or person) to worry about as they continued on their quest. As they did, they watched as their bodies slowly returned to visible status. The spell wore off just in time to avoid detection. Now, it was time to find Mayor Hull and get back to The Land of Fenton.

"Let's go, Walter!" Gabriel said with a smile.

"Right behind you!" Walter replied.

Marge sat at her desk, pretending to be busy when she heard a knock at her office door. Abram stood on the other side of the door. He had to remind himself to be careful. "You are Mort Canton. MORT. CANTON." Abram repeated over and over again.

Marge couldn't hear his words. She looked back at the door after tidying up her desk. She assumed it was her boss, so she called out in a sweet tone, "Come in!"

To her surprise, however, she saw Mort standing there holding a bouquet of flowers. "Hello, Marge!"

"Mort!" Marge exclaimed, caught off guard by his arrival.

"Happy anniversary, my love!" He stepped into the office.

Marge tilted her head. She had no idea it was their anniversary. Typically, in Harmony, no one held celebrations. Mort, however, always insisted on celebrating their anniversary, much to Marge's disgust. She was not about to let her husband know of her disdain. She stepped closer to him after getting up from her desk. "Oh, wow! You are too sweet to remember our special day! And knowing how busy I am!" Marge said falsely. She leaned in with a smile, but Mort blocked it. Marge's attempts at a kiss with Mort were never rejected.

"Oh, sorry! Don't get too close. Gretel's at home sick. I may have caught it. I was able to break away from her for a moment."

Marge nodded, "Well, the flowers are beautiful." She took the flowers and placed them on a table behind her. "Thank you." She turned to walk back toward her desk. However, she could tell he wasn't leaving and turned back after putting the flowers down. "Was there anything else, hon?"

"Well, I was wondering if I could see the place? You know, see things that may be on display? Like, the oil canvas painting we donated?" Mort said with a smile.

Marge squinted her eyes suspiciously. "Why would you want to see that?"

"Well, you know, it was a part of our lives for many years." Mort said with a chuckle.

"That's true. Well, regardless, it's not up to me. Only Mayor Hull can arrange viewings for items like that. He owns it after all. It's in his office." Marge replied.

"Oh, shucks. Well, okay," Mort groaned. "I just miss that thing."

"Why?" Marge pressed him.

At that moment, a voice behind Mort spoke softly.

"I can show him, Marge."

Mayor Hull appeared in Marge's office. "Come with me, Mort." Norm Hull and Marge exchanged looks. "Marge, would you mind running down to Purchasing?

There's a meeting going on I'd like you to sit in on for me. It shouldn't take more than an hour or so."

Marge picked up one of the flowers on her desk, smiled, and sniffed it. "Of course, Mayor Hull." She grinned and Mayor Hull winked at her.

Her husband then left her office with Mayor Hull. As soon as the two were out, Mayor Hull led them toward his own office.

Abram whispered softly as he discretely touched his watch, "So, the oil canvas painting is in your office, Mayor Hull?"

Mayor Hull stared at him, "That's what I said, and what your wife said. Are you hard of hearing, Mort?"

"Nope. Just wanted to confirm."

"I see." Mayor Hull replied with a raised eyebrow.

CHAPTER FORTY

Harmony's Outlaws!

Gretel ran down Elm Street as fast as her legs would carry her. At that moment, however, she had no idea where she was going. She only knew she was running and running far, far away. As she ran, she could hear her heart beating in her ears. She knew in her heart she would never be allowed to return home. She would be banished from Harmony forever. She felt like one of those outlaws she'd seen on television. Was this how her mother felt when she was banished from The Land of Fenton? Where does someone who is banished from Harmony go? Not back to The Land of Fenton, surely?

For a moment, however, she started feel so guilty for running away. Maybe they would help her. Were her parents always this evil? They were evil to Gabriel, sure. Mort showed his true colors to her when her blond hair began to show. However, what about her mother? She was always nice to her, right? That's when she began to remember what happened a year ago when she first learned about the oil canvas painting...

"So, Gabriel's part of The Land of Fenton, too?" Gretel asked as Marge threw the sheet back over the oil canvas painting. "Is he a Dagger-Bagger?"

Marge shook her head. "No. He's not a Dagger-Bagger. But yes, he's from The Land of Fenton." She turned to walk out of the room with her daughter and closed the door back and locked it. "But, Gretel that's why we can't ever let him inside this room. Mayor Hull can never know he exists."

"I don't understand. How did he end up here? With us?" Gretel asked.

"That's not important, Gretel. He is an ugly, disgusting child. And you are my beautiful daughter. That is all you need to know," Marge said ignoring her daughter's questions. She ran her hair through Gretel's brown hair.

"But…" Gretel continued.

"Not another word on the subject!" Marge hissed. "I only showed you this room because you happened to catch me in here! Is that understood?" She then grabbed her daughter roughly by the wrist.

"Ow! Mom!" Gretel cried out.

"Is it understood, Gretel?" Marge said with a raised eyebrow.

Gretel sighed and nodded, "Yes, Mom. It's understood."

"Very good. Remember, Gabriel's not one of us. He's not a true resident of Harmony. He's pathetic," Marge said as she forcefully withdrew her daughter's wrist, making it bounce off Gretel's chest.

Gretel simply nodded. She sighed and walked down the long corridor and back into her room. She kept the door cracked, however. She watched her mother move from the third door room and into the master bedroom. She put a code into a safe and picked up a piece of paper. She smiled wickedly as she read it. Gretel saw her put in the safe's lock code, taking time to memorize it.

Marge walked back into the living room. Gretel knew Gabriel was in his small, windowless bedroom because he wasn't allowed anywhere else. For the first time in her life, she felt sympathy for her cousin. And for a moment, she felt her heart ache for the first time ever for someone other than herself.

A single tear fell from Gretel's eyes. "Poor Gabriel. Poor Gabriel, indeed." She knew in her heart that no one deserved that sort of pain. It was at that moment, she decided she didn't want to be a Dagger-Bagger, or a Canton, if it meant treating someone so terribly.

However, she would never tell anyone in her family the things she felt or saw...

If you asked Marge about that day, she probably never gave it a second thought. However, Gretel vividly remembered it. It was the first moment she began to realize her mother was a monster. She felt sick at her stomach, but knew she had to focus on the future and not on the past.

Gretel continued to run. As she neared the end of Elm Street, she suddenly put the brakes on her feet. "Oh, no!" Gretel screamed as she reached a parked car on the side of the road. After looking in the side mirrors she caught a glimpse of her hair. Her brown hair was now completely blond! "What am I going to do now?" Gretel asked herself.

She took off running again, but this time she ran toward Harmony's Municipal Building. She knew only one person could help her: Gabriel. Hopefully they were still in Harmony. She tried to keep from crying as she neared the intersection leading to her destination. "What would Gabriel do in a situation like this?" Gretel asked herself as she grew closer and closer to her destination.

Once again, her feet suddenly put on brakes. "Oh, great! More Dagger-Baggers!" she exclaimed, taking a moment to catch her breath. There were at least ten of them lined up all along the building's steps. There was no way she was going to be able to get in unnoticed, especially with her new full head of blond hair. A car pulled up outside of Harmony's Municipal Building and parked. Gretel moved to crouch behind it while she waited to make her next move. She took a moment to catch her breath.

Walter and Gabriel heard Abram's voice from their watches. Soon after, they were hot on Abram's trail. They once again recited the spell to become invisible as they traveled behind Abram and Mayor Hull. Abram followed Mayor Hull into his large office. Gabriel and Walter waited outside with the key they stole from Gus as they listened for an earlier agreed-upon signal.

Inside the office of Mayor Hull, Abram took a seat, still in his Mort Canton disguise. Mayor Hull poured a cup of coffee for the two of them. "Well, Mort, I must say you're quite the romantic." He smiled as he handed the cup of coffee to Abram.

Abram clutched the cup in his hand but was careful not to take a sip. He wasn't sure if it was poisoned. "Thank you. I like to think I'm the last romantic man in Harmony," he replied.

Mayor Hull walked back to his desk to take a seat. "You know, it's funny…" he began.

"What's funny?" Abram asked as he continued to pretend to drink the coffee.

Mayor Hull waved his hand, as if it wasn't a big deal. "Oh, it's nothing. I was just shocked to see you here."

"Really, why?" Abram asked.

Mayor Hull shook his head, shrugging it off.

"Oh, come on. Tell me, please! Why were you shocked to see me here?" Abram begged.

"Well, okay!" Mayor Hull chuckled, "I was out campaigning this afternoon and stopped by your place on my way back here."

Abram swallowed heavily in his throat as he stared at Mayor Hull. He didn't reply.

The Mayor continued, "Yes. You made a big deal about how your daughter, Gretel was sick, and you weren't able to celebrate your anniversary. Isn't that funny?" Mayor Hull shook his head and let out a laugh.

Abram began to panic, scrambling to come up with anything to say. "I suppose so. But you see, as soon as you left, I realized how silly I was being. Gretel can take care of herself. She's a teenager!"

Mayor Hull sipped his coffee, giving a sly smile. "Don't you want your coffee, Mort?"

Abram shook his head, "I guess I'm not very thirsty."

Walter and Gabriel could hear through the walls. "What if he gets caught? We have to save him!" Gabriel whispered to Walter.

"Hush, my boy! Trust he can do this!" Walter said holding up his hand to quiet him.

Mayor Hull looked back at Abram for a long time and shook his head. "I make you nervous, don't I, Mort?" He squinted his eyes.

Abram nodded, "Well, I didn't expect I'd be on trial for visiting my wife," he said with a nervous chuckle.

"Good point," Mayor Hull laughed. "Your wife should be able to see any visitor she wants, right? Her husband, or otherwise." He winked again.

Abram looked to his left and to his right. "So, about the oil canvas painting?"

"What about it?" Mayor Hull asked.

"You said I could see it when we were in Marge's office," Mort pointed out. "I'd like to see it again, please."

Mayor Hull pondered the request for a moment, "Hmm, I did say that. Didn't I?"

Abram nodded. "Yes. Don't forget it was in my home for many, many years."

"Well, I suppose you could see it for a moment. Just to know it's in safe hands," Mayor Hull snickered. "Plus, I'm feeling generous today."

Abram stayed seated as Mayor Hull pushed a button discretely under his desk. Abram watched as a painting of Mayor Hull suddenly was lifted into the ceiling above and another one appeared in its place, the familiar oil canvas painting! It was so close to him, yet so far. He saw all the familiar sights: Walter, himself, his daughter, Fern, Matthew and Eden, and of course, the late, King Shamus. He took a moment to appreciate it. "Extraordinary!" Abram exclaimed. "There it is!"

There was the signal. The two nodded at one another, and Gabriel pushed the key into the slot and slowly turned the door handle hearing the click.

"We're in!" he whispered.

"It's show time!" Walter smiled.

Gabriel pushed the door open, and they entered the office.

CHAPTER FORTY-ONE

Messages Failed

Mort paced in his living room after kicking his daughter out over an hour ago. He couldn't understand why her hair was now blond. Was she working with Gabriel and the enemy all along? That wouldn't explain why her hair turned blond, would it? He sighed heavily as he grabbed his cell phone and frantically dialed Marge's work number. It rang and rang but there was no answer.

"Ugh! Marge!" he screamed into the mouthpiece.

He continued to pace around the living room as he bit his bottom lip. How could he reach his wife and quickly, too? He tried to reach her on her cell phone, but that number also rang and rang with no answer.

"I guess I will have to send her a text!" he griped. Mort always hated to send text messages. "Call me! Emergency! Gretel has left!"

Mort would never know it, but Marge wouldn't receive his message. Abram snatched her cell phone before leaving her office.

At that moment, there was a loud banging on the door. Mort, shaken with fear, let out a scream. He quickly calmed himself. "Mort, man, get a hold of yourself. It's probably Gus." He rushed to the door and opened it.

A tall and armed man spoke loudly to Mort, "Are you Mort Canton!?"

Mort nodded.

"I'm afraid you'll have to come with me. We have reason to believe you've been harboring not one, but two blond children."

Mort started to wave his hands. "No, well, yes, but, see, one isn't mine. And the other, I kicked her out."

The man raised an eyebrow, "So, you let two criminals out into Harmony?"

"Well, I…" Mort replied, his nerves shot.

The man pulled out some handcuffs. "I'm afraid you'll have to come with me. You'll be banished from Harmony for good."

Before Mort could react, he felt his hands cuffed together. "No! But I'm innocent. I'm innocent…"

Mort would soon find out where banished residents of Harmony were sent. Mort was no longer welcome to live in a place he and others found so harmonious.

He would never be heard from again…

Gretel heard murmurs of armed Dagger-Baggers talking about a shift change so she looked up from behind the parked car. "This could be my one and only chance!" she said with a heavy sigh. The sun had long since set, and it was very dark and very cold.

Before she decided to move in, her cell phone chirped from inside her pocket. She pulled it out to see a text message from her brother, Gus. "Help! I got locked in a closet and separated from the others."

Gretel read the message twice, wondering how she could help him. She tried to call Gus back, but it went to voicemail after a few rings. "Great!" she groaned. "What am I going to do now?"

Shortly before 11 o'clock, when the shift change began, Gretel moved into position. She noticed there were no Dagger-Baggers in sight so she moved as quickly but quietly as she could. "It's now or never!" she exclaimed as she moved toward a side door.

"Hey, you! Stop!" she heard in the distance as a Dagger-Bagger blew a whistle. "We will attack you, Miss. Stop where you are!" Suddenly, there were Dagger-Baggers in sight. There were many, many Dagger-Baggers, in fact.

Gretel moved through the quad toward Harmony's Municipal Building. She remembered Walter talking about a Creator that was powerful and the leader of all things good. She quietly spoke out loud. "Please protect me!"

As she ran, Gretel heard whistles and warnings given again. "Miss! Stop right now!"

She continued to run as fast as she could. Suddenly, as she looked back, she saw arrows being shot in her direction. Fortunately, each of them missed. She recognized these arrows. They were the same ones she was trained to use in school when preparing to become a Dagger-Bagger. They were nonlethal, but very effective at taking down suspects.

"Run, Gretel!" she told herself out loud as she ran faster than she ever ran before. She almost felt like someone else was carrying her. Something more powerful than any force she'd ever known. Was this the Creator Walter was talking about? Gretel finally reached the side door and tugged it. She heard the hollering of the Dagger-Baggers getting louder and louder. The whistles were deafening, too. The more she tugged she realized the door was not going to open. "I'm not going to make it inside!" Gretel cried.

Suddenly, when all hope looked lost, Gretel saw a window just to the left of the side door. The window was very small. Gretel could probably barely fit. She looked back, seeing the Dagger-Baggers were less than three hundred feet away. If she wanted to try to go through the window, it was now or never. She knew what she had to do. She stepped off the doorstep and breathed out slowly before kicking the window with her foot. It shattered to bits, making a loud crashing noise.

"Alright, Gretel! Here goes! Gabriel is brave, and so am I!" With that motivation in her heart, Gretel breathed in, and then out through her nose. She jumped through the broken window and into the building.

Now the question was how she would find Gabriel and her brother, Gus?

CHAPTER FORTY-TWO

A Question

Walter was the first to spot Mayor Hull, seated at his desk. Gabriel hung back in the entryway for a moment to make more of an entrance.

"Surprise, N.H.!" Walter said as he smiled at his adversary.

"What the…?" Mayor Hull replied, completely caught off guard by what he saw. Walter used his years of combat skills and gave a quick kick to Mayor Hull's wounded right rib, sending him falling out of his chair and plummeting to the floor below.

Abram watched from the seat as his friend who was normally against magic suddenly produced his sword out of thin air. "Whoa, alright! Walter!" Abram cheered.

Walter then nearly drove the sword into the right rib of Mayor Hull, but Gabriel stopped him.

"Wait!" Gabriel shrieked. "Not before I get the answers I want!"

Mayor Hull looked at Walter and Gabriel, terrified. He then turned and watched in horror as Abram morphed back into his original form.

Mayor Hull coughed and tried breathing again. "I knew it was you! I knew it was you!" The anger in his voice raged, making him huff. He'd been out-witted by a child, again!

"What is it you want, Gabriel?" He coughed again. "What, what?" Mayor Hull asked as he looked at Gabriel.

Gabriel looked at his uncle and confidently asked, "Where are my parents?"

Mayor Hull looked at Walter, Abram, and then at Gabriel. "I told you that day in The Land of Fenton. I don't know what happened to them! They disappeared!"

"I don't believe you!" Gabriel shouted.

Walter lifted Mayor Hull up and put him back in his desk chair. Walter, again, used magic to produce a rope that he used to tie him to the chair. "Don't even try to move!"

Mayor Hull glared at the three, "Let me go, you fools! I told you, I don't know where they are!"

Abram suddenly looked at Walter and Walter hung his head. "Abram, it's time the boy knew the truth."

Gabriel spun around, "What? You mean you two know what happened?"

Abram shook his head, "No. I know. I only just told Walter a few months ago. I was promised by your grandfather to keep it a secret."

"Please, Abram, I respect your loyalty to my grandfather, but I have to know!"

Abram sighed heavily, "You don't understand! It's just so complicated. So very complicated…"

Matthew and Eden Mason finally reached The Land of Fenton. They were blessed to be reunited with King Shamus.

"Don't worry about me, my son," King Shamus declared. "I have twelve years of invincibility in this form."

Eden nodded as she heard her father-in-law's words.

"But…" King Shamus continued. "I worry about you two." He sighed heavily. "Your brother won't give up, Matthew."

Matthew shrugged off his father's fears, "Father, we will be fine. We have to be here to raise Gabriel. We have to ensure Gabriel gets the best education as a Wizard."

King Shamus shook his head. "I'm afraid that won't be possible. He won't be going to Fenton Academy. I have already taken steps to have him moved to Harmony. Walter and Abram took him to your sister's, Eden. I asked them to do this when I came to find you two."

Eden began to tear up, "To Marge's? But why?"

King Shamus held his head low, "Because as long as N.H. is around, he's not safe here. Remember he is already marked with his blond hair and blue eyes. With N.H. still out there, you two aren't safe either."

Matthew felt his heart hurt inside his chest. "But Father, will we ever see him again? How do we even know if Marge has changed her ways?"

"Yes, you will see him again. I have my own portal if anything should go wrong! But as far as you're concerned, there's only one way to ensure that you are safe!" King Shamus insisted.

"You don't mean?" Matthew asked, pleading to his father for anything else.

Eden grabbed the hand of her husband. "Matthew, he's right."

They continued on their journey back into The Land of Fenton until they reached The Land of Fenton's Royal Castle. Matthew, Eden and King Shamus were quiet for a moment. None were thrilled with the idea, but all were in agreement that it was the only way to ensure N.H. did not overtake the throne.

"I'm sorry. I wish there was another way." King Shamus responded sympathetically.

Matthew knew his father was right, but it still wasn't easy to hear. "But what if something happens to you after the twelve years?"

King Shamus hopped off his throne and looked up at his son. "Pick me up, my son."

Matthew knelt down to pick him up. "In life or death, we will always be together. We will be together in our hearts. For as long as there is love in The Land of Fenton, there I will be also!"

Eden walked over and joined their little circle. "Should we do this now?" Eden asked, wiping a tear away.

King Shamus nodded, while sitting in the hand of Matthew. "That would probably be best. Yes."

The three walked out of the castle and into the carriage that was waiting for them. It was driven by magic, not animals. "I never even got to say goodbye to Gabriel," Eden said with a heavy sob.

"I know," Matthew replied as he held her from inside the carriage. "But we will see him again one day. "We have to believe that. You know this isn't the end. Our Creator will protect us!"

Matthew looked out ahead, hoping he could believe what he told his wife. The truth was he was more afraid it was the beginning of the end.

CHAPTER FORTY-THREE

Faith Park

King Shamus hopped out of the carriage at Faith Park and Matthew and Eden followed him into the beautiful place. There were waterfalls, orchids, water lilies, magnolias, roses, and animals of every type, all living in harmony together.

"Wow! This place is beautiful. I remember coming here when I was a child!" Eden exclaimed as she looked around. "I used to bring my pet rabbit, Jasper, here."

Matthew nodded as he took time to appreciate the surroundings. "I agree. Absolutely incredible."

King Shamus hopped on top of a boulder nearby. "I thought so, too. I wanted this to be the place so you could at least enjoy…" King Shamus couldn't continue his sentence.

Eden grabbed the hand of her husband again. She held on tightly. For a moment, she didn't want to let go.

Matthew tried to be brave, "It's okay, Father. We understand what has to happen."

King Shamus nodded slowly.

"We know we will see him again someday. When the time is right, he will come back for us," Eden echoed.

Eden and Matthew walked further into the park as King Shamus watched them from the boulder.

"You are very brave. I love you both." King Shamus said softly. A fly flew above his head, but he ignored it. Suddenly, being with his loved ones felt more important than feeding his stomach.

Matthew smiled at his father, "Thank you for teaching me everything I know, Father."

Eden bent down to kiss her father-in-law, "Thank you for ensuring Gabriel's safety." She silently hoped that her sister's wicked ways had changed. She had no way of knowing how wrong she was and just how bad things were in Harmony. "Goodbye for now, Gabriel." Eden softly whispered.

With her hand still in Matthew's, Eden began to recite a spell. Matthew joined in. King Shamus struggled to watch, but he kept his eyes on the scene the entire time. He watched as his son and daughter-in-law slowly became statues in Faith Park. Their former flesh was replaced by marble.

"Goodbye, my son. Goodbye, Eden." King Shamus said as he bowed his head. He hopped off the boulder and turned to hop away. He looked at Eden and Matthew one last time before going inside the carriage.

"I know N.H. will know about you being here eventually, but with this spell he cannot bring you out of this state. Nor can he remove you from Faith Park either. Only the love of your son can break the spell." King Shamus sighed quietly as he rode back to the Royal Castle.

While inside the carriage, King Shamus felt like he lost his entire family in one day. His son, daughter-in-law and now his grandson were gone. His other son was still wicked and would never stop in his quest to take over The Land of Fenton. This made his heart ache terribly.

Later in the evening, Walter and Abram returned from Harmony. They hung a second oil canvas painting up inside the cottage at Walter and Abram's. This would be the second portal for emergencies only.

The two then returned to the Royal Castle to deliver the news to King Shamus. He was sitting down for his dinner. They were initially a bit shocked to see King Shamus, however.

"Sir, what happened?" Walter asked.

Abram touched Walter's shoulder, hoping he'd drop the question. Walter knew something was amiss as Abram warned him earlier something might happen to King Shamus, Matthew, or Eden. "Please! Hush, Walter."

Walter nodded, and the two men knelt before their leader. They stood and then joined him at the table.

Abram explained how everything went down to King Shamus. "We left Gabriel on the doorstep, just as you requested."

"Good," King Shamus said with a sigh. He stirred his bowl of flies but didn't say much more.

Walter continued, "But we have to point out to you, Harmony is extremely weird. It's all about sameness. All the same houses. The cars. The place is really creepy. They even have a mayor advocating for these things."

King Shamus just nodded. He didn't even hear anything they were saying. "Uh huh."

Abram turned to King Shamus, "Need to talk, sir?"

King Shamus sighed, "No. Just a long, long day."

Abram leaned over toward King Shamus and whispered, "So, does that mean?" The former advisor didn't elaborate, however.

The King simply nodded.

CHAPTER FORTY-FOUR

Forever Silenced

Gabriel stared at Abram. "But why not tell me before?" He shook his head, "I don't understand. Why, Abram? Why?" He felt betrayed by his own godfather.

Abram teared up a little, "Gabriel, you weren't ready to save them. But now, now you can!"

The young boy nodded. His parents were still alive, at least in some form. All he had to do was return to The Land of Fenton to find them!

Abram turned his attention to Mayor Norm Hull. He pulled the sash off his robe, and Walter pulled the sash off his. They tied the man down to his chair even more than with the ropes produced by Walter moments before.

"Ha! I can break free from this in time!" Mayor Hull scoffed.

"Not so fast!" Walter replied as he finished tying the man down. "There's a reason we used the sashes from our robes." He then produced a sword after reciting a spell.

Mayor Hull tilted his head, confused.

Abram smiled, "There's magic within these sashes. You won't be able to break free for at least two-day's time. And in that time, we will be long back in The Land of Fenton."

"Face it, you lost this time!" Walter added with a smile.

Mayor Hull struggled to break free. Each time he pulled, the sashes pulled back, tightening their grip on him. Then, he looked beyond Gabriel, Walter, and Abram and began to smile. He started to laugh wickedly.

"And why are you happy all of a sudden?" Abram asked.

Mayor Hull gestured with this head away from the oil canvas painting.

Gabriel moved out of the way and turned to see Marge in the doorway.

"Gabriel, you might be able to keep him from getting to The Land of Fenton today. But how about me?"

Gabriel shook his head. "I can stop you. Just like we stopped N.H.!"

He looked at his aunt for a moment. He knocked her out of the way with a quick kick to the leg and watched her fall onto the floor below. He smiled to himself. He was proud of all his martial arts training he learned from Walter. Marge grunted in pain. "And I did it without magic! I did it with faith!" Gabriel said to her in excitement. He took hold of the sword from Walter and tried to use it on her, but Marge cried out. This time, she was defenseless. She couldn't rely on Mayor Hull to recite a spell.

Marge hollered, "Gabriel, wait! Please! We could do so much evil together!"

Gabriel laughed, "Are you seriously asking me to work with you after all those years of neglect and abuse? Plus, evil isn't in my heart, it's in yours, Aunt Marge!"

Marge climbed back to her feet. She limped a little as she struggled to find her footing. She was still hunched over as she scowled at her nephew. "I was never evil to you! I always fed you. I gave you a bed and a beautiful bedroom!"

Gabriel raised his eyebrow, ready to respond, but he heard a loud scoff from behind his aunt. He immediately recognized it to be Gretel.

"Mother! You are such a liar! You always mistreated Gabriel! And I always looked the other way. I even took up for you. I kept your secrets. Well, until today, Mother! That ends now!"

Marge approached Gretel, slowly. She gasped when she saw her daughter's blond hair. "Gretel! What happened to your hair! You're hideous!"

"Let's just say, I found my true heart!" Gretel turned and winked at her cousin. Gabriel winked back. She moved closer to the middle of the room.

Gabriel smiled. This wink made his heart feel full, and he took a step closer to Marge, trapping her in the middle. Marge looked to her left and then to her right. "Ugh! I never liked kids. Well, except Gus! Where is he? I know he would never double cross me!"

Gabriel grunted, "Well, you're right about one thing. He's locked in a closet around the corner, and I have the key." He dangled the key in front of his cruel aunt, just out of her reach.

Aunt Marge reached for the key. "Give that to me!"

Gretel, hearing the news about Gus for the first time, looked at Gabriel in shock, "Gus was playing us all along?"

Gabriel nodded. "I'm afraid so, Gretel. I'm so sorry."

Marge looked at her nephew and then at her daughter. "I can't believe you are joining his side. I knew you were trouble ever since the day you were born. You were always the weak one! Always!"

Gretel looked at her mother and pursed her lips before speaking, "I am stronger now, Mom. I'm much stronger. All thanks to Walter, Abram, and Gabriel."

Marge laughed for several moments, "Please. Don't give me an ulcer from laughing so hard."

Abram and Walter approached Marge from one side of the room. Gretel joined Gabriel on the other side. Marge was now surrounded by people who could defeat her.

"Believe me, Mother, I'm much stronger than you think!" Gretel smiled, continuing.

"I highly doubt that," Marge said with an eye roll.

Walter stepped up behind Gretel and touched her shoulder. He whispered into her ear, "You're doing great. Don't let her intimidate you, Gretel."

Gretel nodded as she suddenly got a boost in her confidence. She let out a deep sigh, "Well, you always boasted that you'd never let a certain spell get out of your hands. But you didn't know one thing! Your daughter knows the combination to your safe."

"What are you talking about, Gretel?" Marge asked.

Gretel reached into her back pocket and pulled out something very familiar to Marge. In her hand was the spell reversal for teaching animals to speak. "Look familiar, Mother?"

Marge's brown eyes suddenly turned even darker. "Oh, my goodness! Gretel, give that back!"

Gretel laughed loudly. "No, Mother! I think it's time you got a piece of your own medicine."

"What do you mean?" Marge asked as she looked back at her daughter. She was more confused than ever.

Marge's daughter looked over the piece of paper and cleared her throat, "Just wait and see."

The others crowded around as Gretel began to recite the spell clearly and slowly. She wanted to get her first spell right. She raised her hands into the air and then pointed at her mother. "You see, Mother, you've always been an evil beast. Now you will be unable to speak like one!"

"What are you..." and suddenly Marge found herself unable to finish. "I'll..." but the words never materialized.

Gretel grinned at her mother. "Oh, and what's this at the bottom of the paper? Can you read this, Walter? Eden's handwriting is just so small."

Walter looked over the piece of paper, "Ah, yes, it says it's permanent."

Marge ran out of the office, humiliated. The only sounds heard were Marge's feet pounding on the ground as she ran out of Harmony's Municipal Building.

The others huddled around Gretel. Walter hugged her, "Good for you, Gretel. I wasn't sure that spell would work on humans. Especially a human who could speak already!"

"She wasn't human, Walter. That's the difference," Gretel explained.

Gabriel walked over to his uncle and patted him on the back as he sat tied up. "You may want to get something for that rib wound. It looks pretty serious." Gabriel pointed out. Abram laughed at his godson's sarcasm.

"You may have won this battle, Gabriel, but it's not over yet!" Mayor Hull uttered.

"I got what I wanted from you, Uncle N.H. so that's all that matters," Gabriel responded.

Walter walked behind the desk of Mayor Hull and lifted the oil canvas painting off the wall. "Now, if you will excuse us, we have to return to the Land of Fenton."

Mayor Hull watched as his nephew tossed a key on his desk, "Oh, you'll need that when Gus gets out of time-out."

Abram turned to Gretel with a smile, "You're coming with us, right?"

"Of course!" Gretel nodded.

Then, the four took off with the oil canvas painting in tow.

CHAPTER FORTY-FIVE

No Looking Back

Walter, Abram, Gretel, and Gabriel quickly found an empty conference room and decided to put the oil canvas painting in there for the time being until they could come back to get it.

"It will be safe in here for a day or two," Walter said confidently.

"Are you sure?" Gabriel asked.

Abram tilted his head, "I agree. I don't think it's a good idea. Maybe we should destroy it."

Gabriel and Gretel looked back at the two men, confused, and uttered in unison, "Destroy it? Why?"

Walter then realized this was the best option, too. "I hate to admit it, but Abram's right."

Abram took the opportunity to relish the moment. "You think I'm right about something?"

Walter rolled his eyes at his friend, "Don't push your luck, wise guy. But, yes, Abram's right. With the pirate ships sunk from the battle, the oil canvas painting is the only way for Dagger-Baggers to enter The Land of Fenton. We have to destroy it as we enter the painting."

Gabriel nodded. They were right. Besides, there was still the painting back in Walter and Abram's cottage. If trouble occurred, they could fix it.

"Evil will always exist as long as the Universe exists," Walter explained to Gretel and Gabriel. "But don't be afraid. You have love in your hearts. Love is the one thing that lasts forever. A wise leader once said, 'Darkness cannot drive out evil; only light can do that. Hate cannot drive out hate; only love can do that.'"

The two cousins exchanged a smile after Walter's profound words. "Always a teachable moment with Walter around," Gretel quipped.

Gabriel looked at the magical oil canvas painting once it was placed before him. "I suppose you're right. We have to destroy the oil canvas painting." He looked around the room. He could hear voices outside. They were running out of time, "And apparently we have to destroy it quickly!" Gabriel pointed to the door, signaling to the others of the voices on the other side. "I can't believe we're going home!" Gabriel exclaimed with such glee.

Gretel looked a tad uneasy and shifted her weight against the conference room table. "Well, I just hope the residents in The Land of Fenton like me."

"Are you kidding?" Gabriel began, "They will love you!"

Gretel smiled, a bit weakly, however, "I hope so, Gabriel."

Gabriel laughed, "We know so! Oh, wow, Gretel! I can't wait for you to meet Fern. You two will become fast friends. She's a mermaid," Gabriel continued, talking really fast as he began telling about everything he loved about Fenton.

"Whoa! Slow down, my boy. Let her see everything you love about The Land of Fenton in her own way!" Walter laughed. "You were able to do that. Remember?"

Abram turned to the others, "It's time, everyone!"

"There's no need to be worried about any of this, Gretel. But just in case, we will all hold hands, okay?" Gabriel told his cousin.

Gretel nodded and smiled. "Thanks. And for the record, I am sorry for all..."

Gabriel shook his head, "All is forgiven."

Gretel's cousin continued to surprise her. His ability to forgive. "Is this something you learned from the Creator?" Gretel asked.

"You have a lot to learn, Gretel," Gabriel replied with a smile.

"Kids, it's time to go!" Walter called out.

"Oh, give them a minute," Abram said with a grunt. "They're saying goodbye to a place, that's, well…" Abram stopped and then shouted, "Abram's right! Let's go!"

The four friends joined hands and stepped up to the painting. Gretel took a deep breath, not knowing what to expect as they touched the painting with their hands and slowly began to step inside. The painting rippled. "How cool!" Gretel smiled. Walter used his free hand to cast a spell on the painting to destroy it. With a powerful, joint leap, the group excitedly left the world of Harmony behind, once again.

His spell allowed them enough time to reach The Land of Fenton but trapped Norm Hull, Gus, Mort, and Marge in Harmony, forever!

CHAPTER FORTY-SIX

Home Again

From the sky above, Fern saw the portal opening and giggled. She splashed her tail wildly. "They're here!" Fern called out to the other mermaids. The beautiful ocean suddenly showcased a magnificent scene of beautiful mermaids and dolphins doing jumps, flips, splashing water everywhere! They eagerly waited for the arrival of Walter, Abram, and Gabriel. It was as if there was a homecoming celebration happening back in The Land of Fenton in anticipation of their arrival.

The four hollered, flying through the air, headed straight for the ground below. Gabriel was reminded of his first journey into The Land of Fenton. He landed in a pile of leaves. This time, unfortunately, they were headed straight for the boardwalk! "Uh oh!" Gabriel cried out until they hit the boardwalk by the ocean. There was a loud thud when the impact happened.

"Oh, they brought a friend! There's a fourth one!" Fern exclaimed. "Standby, everyone!"

Gretel climbed to her feet. "Well, I suppose that's one way to make an entrance." Her hand was hooked to Gabriel's when they left Harmony. However, the landing on the boardwalk separated the group. She quickly ran to Walter's aid fearing the landing must have hurt the old man. "Walter, are you okay?" Gretel nudged him.

"What a ride!" Walter hollered. "I feel like I'm 95 again!" He jumped to his feet with a loud laugh. "Yippee!"

Gretel shook her head and giggled. She then stared in awe as she looked around to see the beautiful ocean. "Oh, my goodness! That's the prettiest ocean I've ever seen!" She could feel the wind hitting her face. She was amazed how nothing about The Land of Fenton was tainted. The forest was preserved, and the ocean showed no signs of pollution. She took time to see all the animals and other beings nearby, too. They all looked happy and everyone seemed to live in, well, harmony. Unlike Harmony back home, which was no true definition of harmony.

Gabriel stared at Gretel as she saw the sights for the first time, instantly remembering what it was like for him. "Wow! You weren't kidding! I can't believe there really are mermaids!" Gretel smiled and watched as Gabriel pointed to one in particular.

Her cousin nodded. "Yep. And this right here is my good friend, Fern. Fern, this is my cousin, Gretel."

Fern swam over and, as usual, splashed Gabriel.

"Hey!" Gabriel yelped. He blushed after the moment happened.

"Oh, hush!" Fern laughed. "You like it!"

Gretel laughed, "I see she teases you worse than I do."

Fern and Gabriel talked for a few more minutes as Gretel looked on. Gretel watched as Gabriel pushed back his hair nervously several times.

After an hour into their reunion with Fern, Walter and Abram yawned, "Well, we are going to head back to the cottage. We are pretty tired from all the activity. You kids have fun." Abram said as he pointed up the path.

"Are you kidding? We should go on a rollercoaster or something! I feel so alive!" Walter yelled.

Gretel turned back, "Thank you, Walter and Abram. I will see you in the morning."

Abram nodded. "Welcome home, Gretel," Abram said with a smile.

Walter stopped, hugged Gretel and then he, too, headed home with Abram.

As they walked away, Gabriel caught a bit of their conversation.

"Admit it, Walter, you love abusing magic when it's absolutely necessary." Abram snickered.

"I do not!" Walter said as he produced new sashes for the two of them. "It is a dangerous, dangerous thing! We could have been caught!" They securely tied their robes again.

"But we weren't!" Abram said with a wave of his finger.

"But we might've been!" Walter groaned, waving a finger back.

"Will you just admit you had fun?" Abram pleaded with Walter.

"Fine! I had a blast! Now, about that rollercoaster?" Walter replied, begging his friend.

Gabriel laughed as he heard them continue to bicker back and forth. "I guess some things never change."

CHAPTER FORTY-SEVEN

Gabriel's Heart

Gabriel woke early the next morning. He walked into the main room of the cottage to spot Walter, Abram, and Gretel, already eating breakfast. He was in a hurry to get out the door and on his way.

Abram smiled at Gabriel. He knew where the boy was going. "Don't you want to at least have something to eat first?"

Gabriel shook his head. "Sorry. Now that I know where my parents are located, I don't want to waste one more moment without them in my life."

Walter nodded. "We understand, Gabriel."

Gretel took a small bite of her food and smiled gently, "Would you like me to come with you?"

"No. This is something I need to do alone," Gabriel replied.

Gabriel opened the door to the cottage and walked outside. He spotted the carriage left behind by his grandfather from his first birthday party.

"Take me to Faith Park," Gabriel told the magical carriage as he climbed inside.

He immediately felt a sense of peace going to find his parents. He knew he was the only one able to break the spell. The only fears he had as he drew closer to Faith Park were what his first words to his parents would be.

Gabriel practiced along the way, "Hey, Mom! Hi, Dad! How are you? What's up? It's me, your son, Gabriel. I probably look a little different, huh?" Gabriel shook his head. All he could think about was how silly he might sound.

The carriage pulled into a beautiful park entrance, and Gabriel's jaw began to drop, in anticipation. "This must be it!"

It was more beautiful than he even imagined. The waterfall inside the park created a peaceful tranquility. The carriage slowly stopped to allow Gabriel a chance to climb out. After doing so, Gabriel heard murmurs among all the animals living inside the park.

"That's the one," a deer declared as he lifted his head from the ground to spot Gabriel.

"He's the one who has come to save our Kingdom!" a trout said cheerfully as it jumped from one side of the stream to another.

Gabriel felt the pressure to live up to their expectations build but smiled anyway. He took another moment to appreciate the park's beauty. There were roses, lilies and magnolias, just to name a few. Every plant life and every animal seemed to live in harmony with the other. It truly was heavenly!

Then, in the middle of Faith Park, surrounded by gorgeous flowers, he saw them: the statues of his parents. The statues were still beautiful despite the years spent inside the garden. Gabriel guessed that the animals in the forest took care of them out of respect for the royal couple. Gabriel approached the statues with a heavy set of nerves, but knew he had to get over that, or he would be doomed to never see or speak to his parents ever again.

"Hello, Father. Hello, Mother." Gabriel said as he reached his mother and father's statue. He gently reached out to touch them. He touched his mother's hand and then touched his father's arm. He still struggled with the right words to say. "It's me, Gabriel." The statues were cold to the touch, but Gabriel felt strangely comforted and soothed by them. He looked up at his father's statue and then at his mother's. He then whispered softly as he felt his heart begin to beat a little faster. "I love you both, and I made it back!"

He didn't know the spell to bring them back. Walter and Abram wouldn't know one either. He was the only one who would be able to bring them out of this state. But how?

He stared at his parents and continued to hold them. He felt his heart begin to beat wildly inside his chest. This time, however, he wasn't scared. "It's safe now," Gabriel said as he looked at the statues. "I'm here."

At the exact moment Gabriel spoke the words, he watched as the grounds began to shake all around. He was instantly reminded of the moment back in Harmony when Walter and Abram first arrived. This time, however, there wasn't a bedpost for him to grab on to for support. He fell to the ground below. Gabriel looked up to see a bright flash suddenly appear where his parent's statues once were. "What the --? Where are they?" Gabriel cried out.

He looked directly at the bright flash and saw a silhouette of two figures, and the flash grew more and more, nearly blinding Gabriel. He shielded his eyes and slowly approached it. He wasn't able to get too close before he was knocked back on his feet again. The light grew brighter as he sat on the ground, still studying the silhouette of the two features.

Then, almost as quickly as the flash arrived, it stopped, as did the ground's shaking. None of the animals seemed to notice what just occurred. Gabriel stood up slowly and dusted off his clothing. He wiped his eyelids as his eyesight took a second to adjust. He took a brief pause to look where his parent's statues were. He was shocked to see something in place of the beautiful marble statues: his parents! He ran toward them, without hesitation.

"Hello, Gabriel!" a woman with pale, blue eyes said.

"Son!" a man with blond hair and similar pale, blue eyes of his own said. Both of their voices were gentle, and each smiled.

Gabriel recognized them instantly from the oil canvas painting. "Father! Mother!"

Eden and Matthew knelt down and wrapped their arms around their son. Matthew ruffled his son's hair as Eden kissed her son on the forehead.

"I have so much to tell you two," Gabriel said as he hugged them tightly.

Matthew nodded as he chuckled softly, "Tell us all about your adventure, my son."

Eden walked with her husband and son, and back into the carriage. "We knew you'd come back one day," Eden said, tenderly.

Gabriel excitedly began to tell the story of how he came back to The Land of Fenton.

The family was reunited once again. Together, their hearts began to beat warmly.

CHAPTER FORTY-EIGHT

A New Family

Over the next six months, Gretel grew stronger through her spell and combat training through the help of Abram and Walter. As she trained, she found her heart grew and grew as well. She also found that by spending more time with Gabriel, her love for others grew, too. His pure heart was contagious.

Walter took it upon himself to act as a father figure to Gretel. He taught her all about the big book. She learned more about the Creator by reading it.

Walter told Gretel one day, "The most important thing our Creator ever taught us is that we can help another person know they are loved and capable of loving." His expression changed when he continued, "But, unfortunately, some people reject the Creator's love and take their own, wicked path."

Gretel knew she wasn't perfect by any means, but she finally felt that she was part of a family. Her Aunt Eden and Uncle Matthew had more love in one finger than her own mother and father ever had. Sometimes she thought about family back in Harmony, but the pains were soon eased when she felt the love from her new family. Although nothing was official, she almost felt that she was adopted into Gabriel's family.

Gretel was also able to make friends easily. She had friends who were animals, friends who were mermaids, and even other Wizards, too. She felt loved. It felt amazing. With such real love all around in The Land of Fenton, she realized that her friends back at Harmony High were never her true friends.

One late afternoon, she and Gabriel were taking a walk along the boardwalk by the ocean. The wind was lightly hitting their faces and making their blond hairs move, too.

Gretel was rather quiet, and Gabriel was talking about his first adventures in The Land of Fenton. Gabriel finally turned to her and asked, "Is everything okay, Gretel?"

She nodded, "I'm fine. I guess I just keep wondering if things would have been different if I had tried to be nicer to you back in Harmony. Maybe you could have avoided the years of abuse from my parents and stopped N.H. from killing King Shamus. Maybe I'm to blame for everything. I didn't speak up, Gabriel!"

Gabriel shook his head, "It's not your fault, Gretel. Besides, we can't think about those days. All we have is the present. For instance, I'm making up for lost time with my parents." Gabriel smiled.

"Aren't they great?" Gretel asked.

"Oh, the best! My dad taught me how to fly a kite last week. My mom is opening a sanctuary for animals. I get to hang out with you, every day. Walter and Abram cook us breakfast each day. Gretel, I'm truly blessed."

Gretel nodded in agreement, "I couldn't agree more. I feel blessed, too." She paused for a moment, "Although, I still think about Mom and Dad." Gretel admitted, in a moment of vulnerability.

"I know you do," Gabriel replied. "It's okay to miss them. They are your family. You're not regretting coming here, are you?" He touched his cousin's shoulder, gently.

Gretel shook her head, "Absolutely not. This is my home. You, Walter, Abram, Uncle Matthew, and Aunt Eden, are my family. I am very happy." She smiled, reassuringly.

"We love you, Gretel." Gabriel gave his cousin a quick pat on the back.

The two cousins continued to walk along the boardwalk. As they did, they passed several mermaids swimming, and Gretel touched Gabriel's arm. She suddenly had a burning question for her cousin. "I have another thing to ask you. But don't be offended, okay?"

"Sure, what's up?" Gabriel replied.

Gretel flashed a big smile, "Well, I have to know! What's the story on you and Fern?"

Gabriel just laughed and looked at his feet below. He shook his head. "Umm…"

His cousin looked at him and shook her head with a quiet laugh, "It's okay. Your body language says it all, Gabriel."

Fern rose from the water and watched the two on the boardwalk. Although Gretel and Gabriel couldn't see her, Fern smiled. She felt her cheeks blush. Then, she slid back into the water, and disappeared as the sun slowly began to set.

CHAPTER FORTY-NINE

Plans Change

It was late into night when he cut through the final layer of drywall with a small razor. The boy was covered in dust from head to toe. Dozens of empty chip bags and bottled waters covered the floor below. Gus had been trapped inside the custodian closet for several days now. He stood back to look at his work. He clutched the razor as he admired his efforts.

"Perfect! The hole is finally large enough for me to crawl through!" Gus smiled.

Gus looked in the custodian closet for a flashlight and turned it on as he began to slowly crawl through the hole. It wasn't easy, but he continued to crawl through the walls until he came across an air vent. He looked through it. He shined his flashlight and saw that it led to a large, empty conference room. The conference room appeared to have been abandoned long, long ago. Gus took a deep breath and with a heavy kick, busted it open.

"Yikes!" Gus cried out as he pushed through. He fell on to the floor of the conference room. He dusted himself off and looked around the room. He headed for the door that would lead him into the hall. He couldn't wait to find his parents and Mayor Hull and tell them where he'd been all this time.

"Yes! I'm finally free from my prison." He smiled and grabbed the door handle.

He thought back to the last few days and still refused to believe his cousin had won this time around. "Wait a moment! What's that?" Gus asked himself as he looked in the far corner of the room. He let go of the door handle as he approached the spectacular object.

He stared and studied it up close. "It can't be!" Gus yelled, "No! Gabriel!"

Gus cried, anger settling in, falling to his knees. The oil canvas painting was gone, and all that remained was its frame. He knew then there'd be no rematch. Gus was bested by his cousin, yet again.

Just as all hope was lost, Gus felt someone gently touch his shoulder. He looked up and saw Mayor Norm Hull. He was walking with a cane and was a shell of the man he once was. He even looked older, somehow. "Hello, my boy," Mayor Hull whispered.

Gus stood from his feet. "Mayor Hull!" Gus said, feeling unworthy next to the man. "You're alive! Where's my mother? My father?"

Mayor Hull smiled wickedly at the boy. "I believe you and I have a lot to discuss." He patted Gus on the back and ushered him out of the conference room, leaning on his cane as they walked.

"But what can we do? The oil canvas painting has been destroyed. The ships were sunk during the battle with Gabriel back in The Land of Fenton. The Dagger-Baggers all came back here out of fear..." Gus rattled on, wanting desperately to say more. "We're trapped in Harmony, Mayor Hull!"

"We'll find a way back," Mayor Hull snickered. "I don't give up that easily! Come along, my new, humble servant. Follow me, Gus."

Gus watched as Mayor Hull walked down the hallway. For a moment, he thought he should walk away, and find his own path. But, instead, Gus followed the supreme leader. He felt a lump in his throat start to form. The two made their way into Mayor Hull's office, and the door slammed shut behind them.

CHAPTER FIFTY

Gabriel's New Adventure

Gretel stood next to her cousin and sighed, dramatically, "Come on, Gabriel, you can do it! It's never too late for a new adventure! Just go for it!"

Gabriel let out a heavy groan. "Okay, fine. I'll do it. But if she says no, I'm blaming you for it!" He snickered at Gretel.

"Fair enough!" Gretel dusted her cousin's shirt. "You look great. Just go out there with confidence."

On his way out the door, Gabriel passed his parents, seated at a table, sipping tea. "Going somewhere?" His father asked, now wearing a crown on his head.

His mother looked up and put her cup of tea down. "Matthew, you're embarrassing the boy!"

Matthew chuckled softly, "You're right. I'm sorry! Give her that Mason charm."

"I will," Gabriel replied. Before he opened the door to leave, he ran back to his parents and hugged them. "I love you both!"

Matthew and Eden hugged their son tightly. "Thanks for saving us! We love you, too," Eden said with a smile.

"You know who he reminds me of?" Matthew asked his wife after Gabriel left.

"King Shamus?" Eden replied. "I see it, too. We are incredibly blessed."

Matthew leaned across the table and kissed his wife. "I'm sure Father is watching us right now and smiling. He'd be so proud of Gabriel."

The two were right. In a place more idyllic than The Land of Fenton, King Shamus looked down and smiled. He was happy his family was together, once again. He turned to the Creator and asked, "What do you think?"

The Creator looked down at The Land of Fenton. He smiled, too, and replied, "It is well, Shamus. It is well with my soul."

Gabriel walked out the door and took the same path he'd taken many times before. He approached the boardwalk a bit nervously. He saw Fern swimming in the ocean with her friends. He walked down the boardwalk. Fern turned his way, too.

"Hey there!" She splashed him with her tail and smiled. "What's up?"

Gabriel shifted his feet. He couldn't figure out the right words. "Uh, hey, Fern! There's this, um, ceremony coming up at the Royal Castle. It's my coronation as Prince of The Land of Fenton."

The beautiful mermaid smiled and nodded, "I'm aware. I have lived here my whole life, silly." Fern chuckled.

Gabriel felt his cheeks fill with a red hue. "Well, I was wondering if you would, you know, um, like to go with me?"

Fern blushed, too. She then looked at Gabriel, "I suppose you know a spell so I could join you on land, right?"

Gabriel nodded. "Yes, I do. But I don't want it to be permanent. I like you, just the way you are, Fern."

Fern's friends made gentle teasing sounds, embarrassing Gabriel further.

Fern splashed Gabriel again. "Well, how can I say no to you, Prince Gabriel?"

Gabriel smiled, "Great! It's a date!"

From the distance, and out of sight, Walter and Abram grinned as they watched.

"I knew he could do it!" Walter said as he looked at the scene unfolding.

"No! You said that he would chicken out!" Abram rolled his eyes.

"Did not!" Walter waved his finger in his friend's face.

"Did too!" Abram's finger rose up.

The two friends bickered for some time. The argument gave Fern and Gabriel the privacy they rightfully deserved.

"I never did thank you for giving me the courage to stand up for myself," Gabriel said to Fern.

Fern shrugged it off but replied, "You had the abilities inside you the entire time, Gabriel."

The sun began to set behind them. Fern looked at Gabriel and gestured her hand, inviting Gabriel for a swim. He quickly agreed. "Wait for me!" Gabriel called out as Fern swam away.

As he dove into the ocean, Gabriel began to wonder what new adventures awaited him and his friends in the future. But, for now, the present was a perfect adventure…

Made in the USA
Columbia, SC
07 July 2019